Over the Wall

The Bean Greene Chronicles

MARK DURRANT

ISBN: 0692275061
ISBN 13: 9780692275061

For my sister Kathryn, the bravest person I know

Special Thanks to Kolby Larsen for the beautiful cover art and to Tiffany Jacobson Porter for her encouragement and her many hours of editing

Chapter I
Caretakers

The wall loomed in the distance, silhouetted in a ghostly moonlight. Bean sat on the edge of the bed, his foot tapping the floor as his mind raced with wonder and indecision at the happenings of the evening. Though the night had now mined its furthest depths, he was sure what he had seen was no dream. Truly, nothing had ever seemed so real to him... as if his whole life up to this singular moment had been but a faded reverie. He had no earthly reason to trust the glowing apparition that appeared before him just moments ago, but her words pierced him to the very core. He knew, from the deepest places within, that what she said was true.

His hand twitched, every muscle urging him to action – the time was now. He jammed his left leg into his jeans, reaching to brace himself against the bedpost as he struggled in the darkness to steer his other leg into the small opening. Making his way out of the bedroom, he instinctively grabbed the backpack he took with him on his many overnight excursions into the forest. He paused a moment upon reaching the doorway, then doubled back for the twenty-two his father had given him for his thirteenth birthday several months earlier.

And now to get Wart. Bean knew well that convincing his cantankerous younger brother to leave with him would be no easy task. Under the best of circumstances, Wart would fight going with him. But in the dead of night, under these conditions, he would surely put up a Herculean resistance.

Bean crept up the worn, wooden stairs and down the end of the long hallway to Wart's bedroom, avoiding the creaks in the old floorboards with an expertise only possessed by a long time resident. The cold doorknob gave a faint whimper as Bean opened the door and entered the room. Moving across the floor, he sat on the edge of Wart's bed and placed his hand on his little brother's shoulder. His father liked to joked that it took an "Act of Congress" to wake Wart, but, to Bean's surprise, he awoke almost the moment Bean touched him.

"What are you doing?" he slurred, with more than a hint of annoyance.

"I want you to listen carefully," Bean whispered. "You need to get up and come with me. We're in danger and we must leave the house right now!"

Wart could see the earnestness in Bean's eyes through the darkness, but after ten years of militantly resisting even the smallest of his older brother's requests, his response was knee-jerk.

"You're nuts! I'm going back to sleep."

Wart rolled over, turning his back to his brother and yanking his covers up to his ears as a defense to any further aggravation. Undeterred, Bean reached and grabbed him hard by the wrist.

"Wart, this is serious! I'm not asking you, I'm telling you. You're coming with me! We can either do this the easy way or the hard way. What's it gonna be?"

Wart, now fully awake and ready to fight, shot up in bed, wrenching back his arm.

"I choose the hard way!"

A sharp, frequent sound, like a horse meandering down a paved road, prevented a full-fledged battle from erupting between the boys. Both were struck motionless by the strange clip-clop creeping ominously towards the bedroom door. An icy chill raced down Bean's spine as the source of the noise became evident. It was the exact sound a deer's hooves would make on the wooden floors of the hallway. The stag was coming for them!

The boys remained in frozen silence as the steps came to a sudden halt. The two looked at each other, then to the door, not knowing what to do. Seconds ticked by - the boys barely daring to breathe. Finally, Bean eased himself from the bed, gently picked up his twenty-two, and tiptoed to the entryway as if navigating a mine field. Drawing his face up to the jamb, he strained to glimpse through the crack who - or what - was on the other side.

Pressing his nose to the door, a thunderous crash sent him sprawling flat on his back, the rifle sliding cruelly under Wart's bed. Stunned from the blow, he looked up to see the moonlight reflecting off of what appeared to be seven or eight silver knives. The tips of the antlers from the stag he had seen at the wall earlier in the day now protruded through the door. As quickly as they had appeared, the silver horns vanished back through the panel, followed within seconds by another booming crash that showered bits of wood onto Bean's chest. He could now see through the portion of the door that had been decimated by the repeated blows - his gaze locked with the soulless red eyes of the stag.

From behind, Wart let out a blood-curdling scream that broke Bean from the beast's hypnotic gaze. He jumped to his feet, grabbing his brother by the arm as he slid across the bed toward the window.

"We gotta get outta here, Wart!"

Another crash. Bean knew it wouldn't be long before the determined creature made its way through. Giving the window an upward heave, he fumbled to deploy the makeshift rope ladder his father had installed as an escape for Wart in the case of a fire. He flung the ladder out the window and helped Wart over the sill and on to the first step. There was no resistance from Wart now, as he scurried out the opening.

Another smash at the door. Bean looked back and saw the stag was now through to its shoulders. One more attempt and it would be in the room. He knelt to retrieve the gun, but the space between bed and floor was too small for even Bean to squeeze through. Retreating again to the window, he reached one leg over the sill as a final, crushing blow laid waste to what little remained of the door.

For a moment, the eyes of boy and beast met again. The stag leapt over the bed, just as Bean moved the last of his body outside the window. He covered his head with his arms, expecting to feel the animal's razor sharp antlers penetrate his body. Instead, another crash. The opening had proven too narrow for the creature's giant antlers, and they had caught violently against the window's frame.

All was quiet for a moment as Bean lowered his arms, turning to find himself just inches from the flaring nostrils of the giant deer. He could feel its hot, acrid breath against his face and then a violent spray of mucous and saliva as the stag grunted in frustration, disappearing back into the room. Bean hurried down the ladder where Wart was waiting on the ground.

"Daddy, Daddy, help! A giant monster is attacking us!" Wart screamed.

Bean grabbed him by the arm.

"Let's go!"

The boys set off towards the small barn located 40 yards off the back of the house. Halfway there, Bean glanced back just as the stag came thundering through Wart's window, hurtling to the ground in an avalanche of antlers, glass, and fur and leaving a gaping hole in the side of the home as if it had been struck by a missile. The boys stopped for a moment, mesmerized by the scene of destruction unfolding behind them. Undeterred by its fall, the stag shook its head back and forth and raised itself off the ground to resume its chase.

Bolting through the barn door, Bean slammed it behind them, swinging the big wooden latch down and barring the door just as the beast slammed its entire force against it, shaking the entire barn. The two scrambled up the ladder into the loft, Bean pushing on Wart's ample behind in an effort to assist his brother up the rungs. Though the barn door was considerably more sturdy than the one in Wart's bedroom, Bean knew it wouldn't be long before the stag made its way through this one as well.

Wart clutched his brother's arm with panicked ferocity. His usual sarcasm now replaced with sheer terror.

"What is that thing, Bean!?"

"I don't know, Wart," said Bean trying to catch his breath. "Some kinda psycho deer on steroids."

Seeing the fear in Wart's eyes, Bean tried to reassure him as best he could.

"Don't worry, I'm not going to let anything happen to you. I'm sure dad will be here with his rifle any second. Besides, we're safe up here. Deer can't climb ladders."

The latch on the barn door proved no match for the creature and, within moments, it gave way, the stag bursting into the barn. A cloud of splinters, dirt and straw rose up past the boys as they shrunk back from the edge of the loft, just out of sight of the animal. The boys could hear its hooves pacing back and forth angrily on the hard dirt floor. The beast was breathing heavily and audible snorts and grunts rose sporadically from directly beneath where the two were hiding.

Suddenly, a low, raspy, terrible voice rose from below.

"I know you are here. There is no escape. Show yourselves now and I promise you a quick death."

The unexpected voice was more than Wart's already fragile nerves could withstand. Releasing his vice grip from Bean's arm, he ran to the large opening in the barn loft and screamed.

"Daddy, Daddy, help! We're in the barn! Help us!"

The stag, upon hearing the commotion from above, moved to the ladder. It pawed angrily at the bottom rungs, not knowing quite how to best approach an ascent. Bean ran to join Wart by the opening, looking out across the yard in hopes of seeing his father. Nothing.

He peered over the loft edge to see the giant deer backing up to the far wall of the barn, its huge flank muscles twitching in anticipation. It took three powerful steps and launched itself into the air towards the loft, barely clearing the landing and smashing heavily on the floor not more than ten feet from where Bean and Wart stood. The momentum of the deer sent it sliding across the wooden planks and crashing into the loft wall. It scrambled to its feet and spotted the boys. The beast towered over them. Its razor antlers scraped the sloped roof of the barn, causing the animal to tilt its head slightly, giving it an even more twisted, deranged appearance. It slunk toward the boys as they backed up against the ledge of the opening.

The deer growled with a fiendish air of victory.

"So, this is the legendary Benjamin James. I must say, you are a bit of a disappointment. I expected a little more of a fight. Still, delivering your head to One will bring me great favor."

With that, the beast lowered its head, pointing the silver tips of its antlers directly at the boys, and pawed its right hoof against the floor like a bull preparing to charge. He had no red cape, but Bean looked to his left and spied a pitchfork leaning against the wall. Lunging for the tool, he pointed it towards the stag just as it began its charge. The worn handle's end lodged at the junction of the floor and the base of the wall, the sharp prongs pointing up at a thirty degree angle. The spikes sunk deep into the breast of the stag, stopping the deadly antlers just inches from where the boys cowered against the wall. The pitchfork penetrating the animal's chest, it let out a horrible demonic shriek, thrashing its body backward. It screamed with a crazed ferocity.

"You little brat! You will pay and you will pay dearly!"

As it was part of Bean's weekly chores to clean out the barn loft, he well knew there was a small pile of dirt and hay located directly below the window. Bean turned to Wart, grabbed him by the waist-band with one hand and the collar of his pajamas with the other, and, mustering all of his strength, managed to hurl himself and his unsuspecting brother out of the barn window. The boys landed hard but unharmed in the straw. Quickly extricating themselves, they ran back towards the house.

It was then it appeared, yet another monstrous stag, seemingly standing guard near the back door of the home, perhaps explaining the absence of any help as yet from Bean's father. It spotted the boys and, immediately abandoning its post, set off towards them. The two turned on their heels and began to run in the only direction now available to them - towards the wall.

Bean's eyes darted back and forth, scanning the dark field for something, anything, but there would be no pitchfork to save them now. His gaze fixed upon the wall. It was their only hope. Not daring to look back, he could hear the pounding of the beast's massive hooves approaching. He knew there was no way they could make it the 100 yards or so before the deer overtook them, but running was now their lone option.

At the moment Bean braced to feel the cold sharpness of the silver antlers pierce his back - a shot rang out in the darkness. Instantly, the deer was knocked off its feet, the momentum of the beast carrying its body colliding into the back of the boys' legs and knocking them to the ground. The clamor settling around him, Bean lay on his back, staring dazedly at the starry sky above him. He let his head fall to the side, only to find himself inches away from the now lifeless eyes of the giant animal. He spun to his hands and knees, scraping at the ground to gain distance from the grisly carcass. Finally collecting himself, Bean cried out to his brother.

"Are you okay, Wart?"

Wart, lying stunned nearby, mumbled feebly.

"I... I guess so."

Bean staggered through the darkness to help his brother to his feet. The boys stood in the field, staring over the body of the stag. Bean looked towards home to see the figure of his father silhouetted against the back porch light. For the second time that day, his dad had saved him with a shot from his rifle.

Any thoughts the boys had of safety were fleeting as a cry from the direction of the barn pierced the darkness.

"What have you done?" shrieked the voice. "I will kill you! I will kill you all!"

Bean knew immediately it was the first stag. Impaling it with the pitchfork had slowed it only for a moment.

His father yelled from the home, "Run boys! Run! I don't have another shot. Run!"

Both the boys and the first stag ran in unison towards the wall, the brothers reaching it just as the stag arrived at its fallen comrade. Bean watched as the animal stopped and nuzzled the neck of its dead companion. It slowly raised its head, its eyes afire with rage, penetrating like its demonic antlers into Bean's soul. Letting out a fierce cry, it bolted with renewed strength toward the boys. Bean turned and pushed Wart up and over the wall head over feet. He then put one hand on the top of the rocks and leapt over. With nowhere left to run, the boys huddled side by side on the ground, their backs against the wall, waiting helplessly for their imminent destruction.

Then, from somewhere in the shadows of the forest, Bean heard a sharp, high-pitched voice.

"Grab the stone! Now!"

Without hesitation, Bean stood and peered back over the wall. He realized he was at the very spot where he had placed his sister's small black crystal earlier that day. He could see it lying on top of the stones, sparkling in the moonlight like a star in the night sky. Reaching for it, he could feel the power of the stag bearing down on him. He snatched the stone and again sank back against the rocks just as the beast began its leap over the wall. Bean braced for impact. He waited and waited. He waited long past the time that the deer should have ended both Wart and him.

At length, Bean uncovered his arms from his head and cautiously turned to look again back over the wall. He scanned the ground. There was no stag. He then looked across the field. Bean's jaw dropped ever so slightly. There was no home.

Chapter 2
Building a Wall

art had long since cried himself to sleep in his brother's arms. Resting his back against the rock wall, Bean stared deep into the forest looming in front of him. He didn't need the moonlight to know this was a very different place than the forest where he had spent so much of his youth, a fact that, to him, was almost as disconcerting as the disappearance of his home.

With hours yet before sunrise, Bean was left alone to his thoughts. His mind drifted to the unlikely events that had brought him to this moment.

He had scarcely been able to enjoy his first day of summer vacation when his father announced that he had a special project.

"Bean," he said, almost apologetically. "You know the old rock wall between the back field and the forest? It's in pretty bad shape. It's actually not much of a wall at all anymore. I want you to rebuild it this summer. I want you to build it two feet wide and four feet high. Every day I want you to gather three hundred rocks, stack them on each other, and rebuild that wall."

Bean was, as any self-respecting 13-year-old would be, distraught at hearing his father's request.

"Build a wall!" he said in a high-pitched whine, just shy of yelling. "That'll take forever. I won't have any time to play with my friends!"

His father looked down awkwardly at his shoes. The family was well aware Bean did not have any friends, unless you counted Wart, which Bean most assuredly did not.

"Listen, son. I know this isn't your idea of fun, but building the wall will be good for you. And when you're finished, you'll be glad you did it. My father had me build a wall when I was about your age. There are a lot of lessons to be learned from building a wall."

"I'm not interested in learning any more lessons. I just finished a whole year of learning lessons in school," Bean said, his voice trailing off into resignation. He knew full well that once his father had decided he needed to build the wall, he would end up building it one way or the other. To argue about it would be a fruitless endeavor.

Recognizing Bean's unspoken submission, his dad moved toward him, placed his hands on his shoulders and gave him a playful shake.

"You'll thank me one day. Really, you will. We'll get started in the morning. I'll show you the ropes and then you'll be on your own."

Bean's resentment grew with the day as he considered the dire prospect of spending his entire summer building a rock wall. When night arrived, he found himself unable to sleep, contemplating the unfairness of his particular lot in life. But, while wallowing knee deep in feelings of martyrdom and self-pity, something very curious happened - at least it seemed curious to him.

As he lay in bed, the anger and bitterness gradually gave way to resignation and then, to his surprise, excitement. After all, he loved to build things. Rarely a Christmas or birthday went by when he didn't get a box of tinker toys, which he would promptly fashion into a magnificent windmill or mighty rocket ship. His years of experience creating fantastic Lego creations would no doubt assist him in his new occupation. Besides, he thought, it wasn't as if his summer social calendar was filled with competing activities. Yes, upon further reflection, Bean realized he was very much looking forward to building the wall. Not that he'd ever let his dad know. He mused to himself as sleep finally overcame him, "It's not so bad really. I mean, after all, how hard can it be to build a wall?"

Bean awoke early the next morning, but not by choice. After nine months of waking up at 6:00 a.m. every day in order to catch the bus to school, his body had not yet become accustomed to the more relaxed sleeping schedule that summer vacation affords. He lay in bed, glancing around the small bedroom he had to himself off the back of the home. He used to have to share a room with Wart, but that was many years ago - before the incident. He generally liked his room except when it rained. It was built as an addition to the main house and in an attempt by his father to save money, the roof was constructed entirely of aluminum panels. That worked out fine for the most part, but when it rained, Bean felt like his head was stuck in a metal trash can with Wart banging on the side of it with a stick.

Contrary to stereotype, Bean was a teenager who demanded the utmost cleanliness in his surroundings. He was never one to clutter his wall with pictures of a favorite sports team or music group. He really didn't have any anyway. In fact, one looking in at Bean's room on any given day would likely never guess it was inhabited by a 13-year-old boy, or anyone for that matter.

Fifteen feet by ten feet, it had all the markings of a spare bedroom one might keep available for the occasional guest. The floor was made of concrete, covered by two large area rugs whose respective colors and designs had no business being placed next to each other. His few possessions of consequence were kept in the drawer in his bedside table; a faded and tattered note from his birth parents and a small black crystal once owned by his older sister Katherine. The lone piece of artwork on the plain vanilla walls was a picture of a little girl walking through a field of sunflowers. The painting was also Katherine's. He left it hanging on the wall when he inherited the room. Because it was a watercolor, the features on the face of the girl were slightly blurred. He'd sometimes stare at the painting and imagine that the little girl was Katherine walking through the fields on her way back home to see him. He tried not to look at it very often.

Knowing his father would soon be anxious to head out to the wall, he swung his legs out of bed and placed his feet on the floor. Even in the summer, the floor was cold in the morning and he hopped to the nearest rug. After making his bed in a manner that would satisfy even the toughest drill sergeant, he hurriedly dressed himself in work clothes. Being the oldest boy in the family, and with no hand-me-downs available, his parents were forced to buy him new clothing. That meant his mother would only purchase clothes for him when either his ankles or his wrists were fully visible to the world. And at those rare times when he did get new things, his mother would buy him shirts or pants that were two sizes too big in an effort to stretch every millisecond out of the period of time between clothing purchases. As such, Bean was consigned to wear poor fitting clothes, except for that magical window of about three months during which the dimensions of his body actually matched the tags on his clothing. He'd long ago convinced himself the general indifference his school mates exhibited towards him, particularly those of the female persuasion, was a direct result of his unfortunate clothing predicament. He struggled to tie the simple rope belt securely enough to fasten his new pants firmly to his hips, without cutting off all circulation to his lower half.

Bean entered the small, quaint kitchen where his mother was busy preparing breakfast. She stood at the sink, her eyebrows furrowed as she scoured a bowl. Her delicate silhouette was framed against the kitchen window which was in turn framed by the black and yellow sunflower pattern of the homemade drapes. She wore a simple blue dress protected by an apron made from the same sunflower fabric.

"Good morning, Ben!"

Bean's mom was the only person that didn't call him by his given nickname.

"I'm making you a big breakfast so you'll have plenty of energy to work on the wall," she said cheerily. Bean guessed this was an effort to dispel some of the sourness she knew he must feel about his summer chore.

Sitting down at the kitchen table, he watched his mother work. She had a gift for making the most scrumptious food out of the limited and simple ingredients inhabiting the Greene pantry. Consequently, the boys ate well, particularly Wart. She felt Bean's gaze and glanced back at him with a warm smile. As she turned back to her work, he wondered how anyone so unhappy could manage to smile as much as his mother did - her eyes conveying a deep sadness that could not be smiled away. There was a brief moment when the morning sunlight struck her long, strawberry blonde hair in such a way that it looked to him as if it were going to burst into flames.

"You know Ben," she said with a sentimental air as she sat down at the kitchen table, "I've always loved that wall."

She took his hand in hers and gazed out the window.

"When your father and I were first married, we'd take long walks through the forest, and when we got back we'd sit on the wall and talk for hours. And when you were a baby, it seemed like the only thing that could stop your crying was to take you out there. You'd sit on my lap and stare into the forest until you fell asleep. I always wondered what you could see in that forest that I couldn't. It's made me so very sad to see it fall apart over the years."

She paused for a moment, as if contemplating her regret.

"But now you're going to fix that, aren't you Ben?" She squeezed his hand tightly.

"Um, sure thing Mom. But I don't know what's such a big deal about a dumb old wall."

"You will someday," she said confidently, reaching with her other hand to gently stroke the side of his head.

Just then, Wart stumbled into the room, groggily rubbing his eyes. The smell of mother's rib-sticking apple pancakes had towed him cartoonishly by the nostrils to the kitchen table. Wart wasn't much to look at as his nickname, unfortunately for him, was fairly descriptive of his general appearance - small and round with a few hairs sticking out the top. And boy could he eat. Even though Bean was almost double Wart's height, Wart would eat twice as much and still be hungry. In fact, the two boys couldn't be further apart on a spectrum of physical characteristics. Virtually opposites in every way imaginable, Bean had concluded that part of the reason he wasn't surprised when he learned of his adoption was there was no possible way he and Wart had swum in the same gene pool, or ocean for that matter.

Bean had long ago convinced himself that Wart's sole purpose in life was to torment him. Though younger, Wart had a decidedly better sense of humor and used it as a weapon to mock his older brother at every opportunity.

"Hello Mother, hello Brother," Wart greeted the two coyly. "What a beautiful day it is. Say, Brother Bean, do you know what I think I'll do today?"

"Eat?" replied Bean, trying to draw first blood.

Unphased, Wart said gleefully, "I think I'll NOT build a wall."

Mother stepped in, "Warren, unless you want to be out there building the wall with your brother, you'd better watch it."

His mother's warning brought Bean a sudden realization of the inequity of the situation.

"Why doesn't he have to help build the wall mom?" he moaned. "It's not fair."

"Ben, when you were eleven, you didn't have to build a wall either," she replied matter-of-factly.

"Yeah Bean," Wart chimed in. "Stop being such an Eeyore all the time."

Before the fight could lead to its inevitable conclusion, with Bean placing Wart in a headlock and Wart being forced to say, "I take it back!" Mother quickly plopped two large pancakes onto Wart's plate. Wart dug in immediately, food taking precedence over teasing his brother. Bean took a breath to complain about Wart being fed first, but was quickly stopped by a knowing look from his mother. She was right. Everyone was better off if Wart's attention was occupied with flapjacks.

Chapter 3
Moses

Of course, Bean was a nickname. Only the cruelest of parents would name their child Bean, or any other vegetable for that matter. His given name was Ben, or more particularly, Benjamin James Greene. The moniker Bean came about when Warren, two years his younger and just learning to talk, uttered the word "Bean" when trying to pronounce the name Ben. Once that came out of darling little Warren's mouth, Bean's fate was sealed, and he would never be referred to as Ben again. Naturally, he harbored a certain resentment towards Warren for giving him the nickname. After all, he thought, how hard is it to pronounce the name Ben, even for a one year old. But he did manage to exact a measure of justice on his younger brother. It was Bean that came up with Warren's nickname, Wart. So, in the battle of nicknames, Bean and Wart considered it a draw and eventually resigned themselves to their respective appellations.

It should also be noted that Bean's first and middle name, Benjamin James, were not chosen by his parents, at least not by his adoptive parents. Not long ago, on his thirteenth birthday, his mother and father ceremoniously announced to him that he was adopted. As might be imagined, hearing such news was heartbreaking for Bean; though, for reasons too numerous to recite here, not completely surprising. His parents then carefully related to him the story of his being left on the doorstep one winter night, wrapped snugly inside a little basket, a veritable Moses washing up on the shore of the Greene home.

Fastened to the coarse blanket that served as his only protection from the harsh, chilling wind, was a simple note that read:

> Please watch over our child.
> He is very special.
> His name is Benjamin James.

Leaning forward, his father continued in a hushed tone, as if divulging a secret.

"I rushed out to see if I could find the person who left you. I followed a set of footprints in the snow that led behind the house toward the forest, but after a few minutes, they just vanished. The wind was so strong it must have erased the tracks almost as soon as they were made. Whoever it was, I'm afraid they couldn't have survived out there for very long. It was one of the coldest nights we've had around here in years."

His mother reached slowly into the pocket sewn into her hand-made skirt, pulled out the note, and handed it to him.

"Ben," she said through glistening eyes, "Just because you were adopted doesn't mean we don't love you as our very own. I want you to always remember that wherever you go and whatever you do, there has never been a mother in this whole wide world who loved her son as much as I love you."

Bean didn't look at the note or his mother. He simply took it to his room and deposited it carefully in the drawer by his bedside.

Bean and his father stood together in the field surveying the battered remains of what used to be a wall. Over the past six years, it had fallen into such a state of disrepair and neglect that it seemed now as if there was not a single stone remaining atop another. Bean remembered once reading a Robert Frost poem in English class called "Mending Wall." He had been required to memorize the first few lines:

> "Something there is that doesn't love a wall,
> That sends the frozen-ground-swell under it,
> And spills the upper boulders in the sun,
> And makes gaps even two can pass abreast."

Bean looked up at his father and said, "Gee Dad, something there is that really does NOT love this wall."

A half smile crept up his father's weather-worn cheeks. Bean loved to make his dad smile as achieving such an accomplishment was a rarity. And to make his father laugh, well, that was like finding a twenty-dollar bill in an old pair of pants.

Even though Bean was adopted, he had the same long, lanky frame as his father. He was already a head taller than most of his classmates, and his dad liked to tease him by telling him he was "growing like Jack's bean stalk." His current "two-sizes-too-big" stage required him to roll up his pant cuffs, a stark contrast to his father who wore denim overalls that didn't quite reach his ankles. The two made quite a pair as they stood side by side in the field.

His father reached over and put his slender but strong arm around Bean, pulling him closer. The two stood staring at the wall for the longest time. Bean would occasionally glance up. He could see his father's brown eyes shimmering in the morning sun. He had never before seen him cry. He began to feel uncomfortable with the prolonged silence but sensed he shouldn't speak. Finally, his father, still staring at the wall, spoke in a somber, solemn manner Bean had never heard before, an invisible weight now pushing on his father's shoulders so he and Bean were of almost equal stature.

"I look at this wall and I see our little family," he began, choking on his words. "We're broken Bean. I'm sorry I've let this happen. I'm sorry that I have neglected our family, and especially you. It's just been so hard since..." his voice trailed off, either unable or unwilling to finish.

Pausing for a moment to regain his composure, he continued with renewed strength.

"This wall needs to be mended. Will you help me mend it, son?"

Not knowing for sure if his dad was speaking of the wall or his family, Bean said earnestly, "Yeah Dad, I'll help you mend it. I promise."

His father smiled warmly.

"I knew I could count on you, son. You have greatness in you. I see it every time I look at you. This will be a day that you and I will always remember. This will be the day that we began to mend the wall."

Bean's father wiped his red flannel sleeve over his eyes, raised his shoulders once again, took a few steps towards the battered wall, and picked up a stone. Each was about the size of a loaf of bread. Some larger stones were already in place at the base of the wall and seemed to have been lodged there since the beginning of time. It was a good thing, too. Even though Bean was large for his age, he wouldn't have been able to move rocks that size. His father began gathering the stones, stacking them on each other and, before long, had completed a two or three foot portion of the wall. He turned to Bean and said simply, "Any questions?"

"I think I've got it Dad. It's not rock-et science."

This time his dad laughed heartily.

"I guess it isn't. I didn't mean to insult your intelligence."

Bean glowed with satisfaction.

"Now, like I told you before, three hundred stones a day, and then you're free to do what you like. I want you to start at the end here, and go all the way to the end of the field over there."

Bean looked to where his father was pointing. The length of the wall neared a thousand feet. Doing some quick math in his head, he figured he could do about 15 feet or so of the wall each day. Leaving out Sundays, it would take about two and a half months. That would leave him a couple of weeks of summer vacation all to himself.

"Well, I'll leave you to it, Bean. Thanks for doing this. It means a lot to me."

His father turned and began walking back toward the home. Half-way across the field, he yelled back to Bean, "Remember, one day, we'll look back on this day and smile."

"Sure thing, Pop. Sure thing."

With his father gone, Bean turned to assess the task in front of him. Most of the rocks he would need were near the base of the old wall, but it quickly became clear he would need to gather some stones from the field in order to complete the job. There were plenty of rocks to be had there as the field had never been cleared for farming. His family's property sat in the middle of the most fertile farmland in all of Missouri, but Bean determined the only crop that had ever grown in their field was, in fact, rocks - rocks and the seemingly never-ending supply of weeds and thistles that seemed to flourish there out of spite. Farmer's had long since given up on the property, which was part of the reason his parents could manage to afford the land in the first place. He figured he'd have to harvest at least 100 rocks from the field every day to meet his 300 stone quota.

After a few minutes of building, he realized the construction of the wall would require more than just stacking stones atop one another. In order to give the wall the requisite shape and sturdiness, he would have to fit the pieces of stone just so. The project would be less like the Legos he had originally envisioned and more like a giant jigsaw puzzle. Already wiping his brow in the early morning sun, he recognized his task would take much longer than he had anticipated.

Not long into his workday, Bean looked up and saw Wart making his way out towards the wall with two tall glasses of lemonade. Wart walked up to him jauntily, greeting him with, "Hi-ya Jolly Greene Giant. I felt so bad for you out here working on this wall that I made you some tasty lemonade. Ain't I a great brother?"

Bean played along, knowing full well his mom made the lemonade and forced Wart to bring it out to him.

"Yes Wart, your selflessness never ceases to amaze me."

"So how goes the wall building Greene Bean?" Wart asked.

Rarely did Wart ever address Bean without using some variation of his nickname. As you might imagine, the name Bean Greene lent itself to much mockery, not just by Wart, but by all of Bean's classmates. Of course, he had been called every conceivable type of bean: kidney, lima, garbanzo, baked, jelly, refried, pinto, and string, to name a few. And he couldn't recall a time walking down the halls at school without someone singing, "Bean, Bean, the musical fruit, the more you eat..." Well, you know the rest. And his last name, Greene, only exacerbated his predicament.

"It goes," replied Bean. "Don't strain yourself watching me."

"Oh, I won't. I don't want to tire myself out. You see, I've got a full day of doing NOTHING ahead of me," said Wart gleefully.

Bean shrugged, trying his best to act indifferent to Wart's barbs.

"Say Human Bean," asked Wart, "Isn't the whole point of building a wall either to keep something out or in?"

"I guess so," Bean replied warily, waiting for the other shoe.

"Well, this wall doesn't look big enough to keep anything out or in, except maybe a turtle. And I haven't seen too many turtles around here."

Bean, sensing an opening, replied coyly, "Well Wart, it just so happens that this wall is a special wall. It's built to keep out all the monsters that live in the forest."

Wart was deathly afraid of the forest and would only go in if it was in the middle of the day, and then only if Bean was near him at all times. Once he was in, his only objective was to leave. Not that there was anything to be scared of, mind you.

Bean practically lived in the forest and had never once seen a dangerous animal, or monster for that matter.

"There ain't no such thing as monsters, you can't scare me," said Wart with feigned courage.

"Oh yeah," Bean replied as he grabbed Wart by the wrist, "Then I guess you won't mind if I drag you into the forest and leave you there by yourself."

Wart's wide eyes conveyed the sudden burst of fear as he struggled mightily to break Bean's grasp, spilling his lemonade on the rocks. Bean half-heartedly held on as Wart eventually broke free and began running towards home.

Regaining what composure and dignity he could, he yelled back, "The only monster in that forest is you, you big freak."

With Wart out of his hair, Bean deposited himself on the newly constructed portion of the wall to drink his lemonade. He looked at his house, then turned back to look at the forest. Between the two, he wasn't sure where he felt more at home. It was likely Katherine was the origin of his love for the forest. His first memories were of long walks with her through the trees and brush, exploring the many wonderful and exciting mysteries the woods held. Now that she was gone, the forest was his best and only friend. He knew every tree and rock, every secret and hidden place. The forest was his kingdom and he was king. When he entered, he felt a sense of confidence and power, as if all of nature was at his command. He felt no fear, even when camping out by himself overnight. In the forest, his imagination was free to make him the man he knew he would never be in the real world. Even at his young age, he sensed the irony that the only time he didn't feel alone was when he was by himself in the woods.

The forest itself consisted of several thousand acres in the lush, rolling hills of south-central Missouri. The majority of the acreage was part of the Mark Twain National Forest, which designation kept the land in its natural, pristine condition, free from the inroads of farming and development. Clear spring-fed rivers and streams, rocky bluffs, idyllic views and shaded trails made it the perfect refuge for a young man desperately in need of an escape from the world.

Most of the forest consisted of expansive stands of short-leaf pine, but there was the occasional grouping of hickory, with a few giant oak mixed in for good measure. Bean didn't like to climb the trees, as he wasn't much for heights. He had started construction on several different tree houses, but quickly found he much preferred his fortresses to be located at ground level. There wasn't much animal activity to speak of, at least not anywhere near his home. Bordering development had pushed the larger animals deep into the safety of the forest, and any big game knew best to stay well hidden. There were plenty of squirrels and rabbits though, and some of the boys in his class enjoyed the occasional afternoon rabbit hunt. He couldn't stand the thought of shooting anything, especially his little forest friends, but he never had to face that particular moral dilemma, as he was never invited to join in.

As the summer days lengthened, Bean came to find he enjoyed the solitude of the work and the proximity to the forest. Some days, without realizing, he would do more than his required allotment of rocks. Aside from the occasional visit from Wart, he was left on his own.

Just a stone's throw from the wall ran a small stream. From his bedroom at night, Bean could hear the faint babbling of the water spilling over the rocks. Most days he would take the sack lunch his mother had prepared and sit alongside the stream to eat. He would stick his feet into the cool water, providing a welcome respite from the oppressive summer heat. Like the water cascading over his toes, invariably his thoughts would flow to Katherine.

There were so many questions. What had happened to her? Most everybody but his mom and dad thought she was dead. All Bean knew was she was gone. But where? Was she okay? Was she in trouble? It might have been easier on his mom and dad if she were dead. At least then they could have tried to move on. But the uncertainty around her disappearance was torturous and cruel. It had almost killed his mother. She had just now, after six years, emerged from the fog of gloom and despair that had enveloped her.

Bean closed his eyes and could see Katherine's auburn hair and porcelain skin as if she were now standing in front of him. He had always been fascinated by her hair, which matched the color and sheen of a polished penny reflecting in the afternoon sun. Sadly, his memories of her disappearance lacked a similar clarity. His recollection of the events was viciously hazy and vague. He simply remembered waking up one morning with his mother and father in a panic, frantically searching the house for Katherine. He could, even now, see the fear in his mother's eyes when she grabbed his shoulders forcefully, pleading to know if he knew where she was.

"Did she say anything about where she might have gone? Think Ben, think! Try and remember! Anything - did she say anything at all?" his mom begged.

He remained silent. He couldn't remember anything. There was nothing for him to remember.

Of course the police were called in, but after several months with no leads, the case was closed. There was no sign of Katherine. There was no sign she was taken. The only thing out of the ordinary was that the back door was found open. As she was fourteen at the time, most everybody figured she ran away. But not Bean.

For several weeks following her disappearance, he all but lived in the forest. During his time there, he would often imagine Katherine was speaking to him. That is to say, over the last six years he had convinced himself it was his imagination. But at the time, he knew it was really her. He could hear her talking to him in the bubbling of the stream and the rustling of the wind through the trees. He would shout out, demanding to know why she left and where she had gone, but he could never quite make out what she was saying. Of course, now that he was older, he knew such a thing was impossible. Still, as he sat every day by the stream eating his sandwich, he found himself listening for Katherine's voice.

Chapter 4
Strange Happenings

The closer Bean got to finishing the wall, the stranger things got. He began to hear a growing, disconcerting chorus of invisible beings whispering to him while he worked in the summer heat. The voices frightened him at first, and he refused to work on the wall for several days, but after prolonged prodding from his parents, he worked up his courage and again ventured out to build.

As bizarre and disturbing as the voices were at first, it wasn't long before Bean became accustomed to the presence of his unseen companions. Naturally, he worried he might be losing his mind. He knew that hearing voices in one's head is not the hallmark of a sane person. He desperately wanted to tell his parents but determined such a revelation would only place more weight on their already burdened shoulders. Besides, he thought, telling them would likely result in countless trips to doctors and psychiatrists. They might even commit him to a mental hospital, and he certainly wasn't very keen on that idea. So Bean decided to just put up with the voices in his head. After all, they weren't telling him to start any fires or to hurt anyone - at least not yet. And what were the voices telling him? Well, they were simply telling Bean, over and over again, to stop building the wall. But he wasn't about to do that now, no matter what the imaginary voices were telling him.

He just couldn't stop. Too much time and effort had gone into his work, and he was now only a week away from finishing the wall altogether. More importantly, building the wall had become more than just a chore for Bean. It had instilled within him a sense of purpose he had never before experienced in his young life. Notwithstanding his suspicion that the recent turn of events had brought him to the very brink of insanity, his progress on the wall brought him great satisfaction and contentment. He loved to sit and look at his handiwork, taking a great deal of gratification from knowing he had built something so big at such a young age.

His father and mother couldn't praise him enough and the wall was often the topic of conversation at the dinner table, much to the chagrin of the attention seeking Wart. Hearing them fawn over Bean was like depriving Wart of oxygen. Wanting to be a part of his parent's acclamation, Wart even offered to help Bean work on the wall, but his enthusiasm waned after about twenty minutes, and he was quickly off to participate in less physically taxing endeavors. Wart knew he could find less labor-intensive ways to get the approval he so desperately craved.

With just a few days of wall building remaining, the finish line lay clearly before him. Even with the now constant barrage of voices plaguing Bean as he worked, he regretted he would soon be done. After all, it wasn't as if there were other pressing matters he was eager to get to. With the dark clouds of school again looming on the horizon, the thought of going back to his regular life, with no more wall, began to weigh heavily upon him.

He would have completed the wall before now but for the fact that he was forced to spend a half an hour or so every day replacing rocks that had fallen from where he had placed them the day before. It seemed no matter how carefully he arranged the stones atop one another, invariably twenty or thirty were back on the ground the next morning. After a time, he became convinced someone was sabotaging his work. Of course his initial instinct was that Wart was the culprit, but he soon realized the effort required to pull off the stunt exceeded what Wart was likely willing to exert, even if it was for a prank at Bean's expense. But who else could it be? He decided the best way to find out was to catch the saboteur in the act. So, armed with a flashlight and his twenty-two rifle, he decided to hide in the forest and find out who it was, once and for all.

His family long since in bed, Bean snuck out to the wall, finding a spot thirty feet into the forest where he was fully hidden from view. He chose the spot due to its proximity to the center of the wall where most of the damage seemed to occur. Nestling in against the trunk of a large tree, he began the wait. Despite his best intentions, it wasn't long until he lost the battle to stay awake. After several hours of slumber, he was awoken by the sound of whispering voices.

"It's okay, he's still sleeping, keep going."

Remaining perfectly still, he slowly opened his eyes and peered at the moonlit wall. Nearby, he heard the distinct thud of a stone falling to the ground.

"Quiet, you'll wake him!" hissed another voice.

Bean stared at the wall in an effort to make out the shadows of the perpetrators against the night sky. When he originally formulated his plan, he hadn't considered there may be more than one culprit and he now began to fear his twenty-two might not be enough protection.

"You two take care of that section and we'll finish up here," whispered yet another voice.

It now seemed to Bean that, for some unknown reason, an entire army had made it their mission to tear down his little wall. Finally, working up all of his courage, he made his move, leaping to his feet and pointing his rifle in the direction of the commotion. Rising, he heard a high-pitched squeal coming from the wall.

"He's awake! Abort, abort!"

Instantly, the bushes to his left and right came alive, bristling with activity. Hurriedly turning on his flashlight, Bean pointed it to the wall, moving it side to side, expecting to catch a glimpse of the evil doers, but he could see no one. Finally, his eye caught sight of something round and small on top of the wall. He pointed the flashlight at the object just as two long furry ears shot straight up into the air. When the light hit the small creature, it froze in fear as its eyes locked with Bean's. After a few moments, it let out a panicked squeak, bolted from its perch and disappeared into the forest.

"A rabbit?" muttered Bean incredulously as he stood there, stunned. "But, where are the people? I know I heard people."

He scanned the horizon with his flashlight, but again, no one. Whomever, or whatever was there, had vanished.

Undaunted by the bizarre events of the prior evening, Bean resumed his work the next day, constructing the wall while pondering the peculiar nature of his late night encounter. Just as he was preparing to place the final ten rocks on the wall before returning home for the afternoon, he was stopped dead in his tracks as the loudest, most clear voice yet, almost shouted in his ear.

"STOP BUILDING THIS WALL, OR I WILL MAKE YOU STOP!"

He whirled around, fists extended in full fighting mode, expecting to see someone standing behind him, but there was no one. Quickly spinning back, he peered into the forest searching for the as yet unseen intruder. Again, no one.

With both fright and defiance, Bean yelled out, "I know you're there, I'm not scared. I'm finishing this wall and you can't stop me!"

Tilting his head slightly while moving his ear forward to hear a response, he was once more met with only silence.

After sufficient time had passed to allow Bean to convince himself he was indeed alone and to calm his already frayed nerves, he returned to his work at the wall, hastily moving the final few rocks of the day in hopes of removing himself as quickly as possible from his current uneasy situation. Bending to rearrange one of the large stones at the wall's base, he again heard a sound, but this time very different than any he had previously encountered. Not a single voice, more like hundreds of tiny little voices. Together they made a conspicuous buzzing sound that grew louder and louder, seeming to emanate from within the wall itself. Moving in closer to examine the source of the hum, he removed a few stones in an attempt to discover its origin. Even before the toppled rocks could reach the ground, his face whitened in terror as he realized the cause of the commotion. He had just uncovered a massive hornet's nest! The air around him quickly blackened as hundreds of hornets rose like smoke from a raging fire. Bean did the only thing he could do – run, but it wasn't long before the swarm was on him and he began to feel hundreds of sharp pin pricks on his exposed skin. All the while he was running and being stung, it was as if he could hear a throng of tiny voices saying, "Get him!" "Don't let him get away!" "I've got the back of his neck!" "We need to stop him!"

Though running faster than he ever had in his young life, it seemed an eternity before Bean was able to cover the few hundred feet to the stream in the forest. Several weeks prior he had dammed up a portion of the stream to make a little pool where he could soak his feet and cool down in the stifling summer heat. Literally making a bee line for the pool, he leapt into the water, making a huge splash. He lay on his back plugging his nose, allowing the remaining water in the pool, just deep enough to cover his body, to protect him. Staying under the water for as long as possible, he came up only for short breaths.

His eyes open, he could see from beneath the water that many of the hornets were still hovering above him, waiting. Finally, the swarm began to dissipate and, when he thought it safe, Bean slowly sat up. Wiping the water from his face, he could see only one hornet now remained. It hovered in front of him for a few seconds and then deliberately flew to within just a few inches of his nose. His first instinct was to duck back into the water, but before he could, the hornet stopped and, to Bean's utter and complete astonishment, looked him dead in the eye and said firmly, "Stop building the wall, or else!"

With that, the hornet turned away, shook its stinger back and forth as if sending one final message, and flew back in the direction of the wall.

Chapter 5
The Key Stone

Bean knew he was beaten. If cuddly forest creatures bent on vandalism and talking hornets with an oddly personal vendetta didn't want the wall to be built, who was he to argue? Besides, the hornet stings covering his body and the mild allergic reaction that came with them gave him sufficient cover with his parents to cease any further activity on the wall. At least for a few days.

"Just when I thought you couldn't get any uglier," said Wart when he saw Bean's swollen face.

Bean countered, "A bunch of hornets made me look like this, what's your excuse?"

"Hornets wouldn't dare touch this masterpiece," Wart replied, framing his face with his hands as if on display at the Louvre.

Notwithstanding Wart's occasional interruptions, Bean relished his impromptu vacation and the desperately needed break from the voices. They had taken a toll on him, even before the hornet attack. His life was hard enough without having to deal with his apparent break from reality. Three days in bed and not a single voice in his head. Not a single bird or adorable little chipmunk threatening him with bodily harm from his window sill. He actually began to feel normal again. Besides, it wasn't difficult for him to become accustomed to being waited on hand and foot by his mother.

At the end of his third day of bed rest, Bean knew his vacation would soon be coming to an end as the hornet stings had now almost fully healed. So, it was no surprise the next morning when his father poked his head into the bedroom.

"Get dressed kiddo. I've got a surprise for you."

Bean dutifully put on his clothes and met his father in the kitchen.

"Let's go for a walk," his father said as he opened the back door, not waiting for a response.

The two walked toward the forest. His dad spoke, "Bean, I felt bad about your accident. I felt responsible, seeing as how I was the one who asked you to work on the wall. I know how hard you've worked. I'm really proud of the job you've done this summer. Anyway, you only had a little bit more to go so, while you've been laid up, I decided to finish the wall for you."

Bean's eyes and mouth widened as he saw the wall had indeed been finished.

"Dad... what have you done?" he almost shouted with a tinge of terror, quickly surveying his surroundings for any approaching hornets.

"I don't understand son, I thought you'd be happy."

Bean stammered, not wanting to hurt his father's feelings, "I... I am happy dad, it's just that... well, the thing is --"

"I think I understand son. You probably wanted to finish it yourself. I should have let you do it. I'm sorry."

Seeing the regret in his father's eyes, Bean replied, "No dad, really, it's okay. Thanks. I mean, it looks great."

He gazed out at the completed wall. It really did look good. After all, Bean reasoned to himself, it wasn't me that finished the wall. He hoped that technicality would protect him from the invisible voices.

The new school year just a few days away and the wall now complete, Bean was eager to spend his remaining free time with his one true love, the forest. Unfortunately, getting there meant he would have to traverse the wall. Of course he could have taken the trouble to walk around it, but that would have been an admission of cowardice not even he was willing to make. It's just a stupid old rock wall, he told himself over and over again. Yet, despite his best efforts, he couldn't help but be leery about even getting near it. Eventually, his affection for the forest overcame his fear, real or imagined, and the next morning Bean's mom packed him a lunch and he started out across the field. About halfway there he came to the conclusion it might be a good idea to bring along his twenty-two, just in case.

It was his practice to enter the forest near the wall's midpoint. He expected to see the usual allotment of rocks knocked off the wall, courtesy of his talking forest friends. To his mild surprise, all of the rocks remained snuggly stacked in place. Perhaps by surprising them in the act, he had dissuaded them from any further mischief.

Coming within a few feet of the wall, his pants pocket suddenly felt as if Wart had jammed a 4th of July sparkler in it. He realized the source of heat was Katherine's crystal, which he kept with him as his constant companion. He hastily pulled it out of his pocket, but could barely hold it for the warmth it was now giving off.

Moving it from hand to hand like one of his mother's chocolate chip cookies fresh out of the oven, Bean stared at the small black rock curiously. When Katherine had given it to him on his seventh birthday, it seemed an unusual gift, but he loved it immediately. He had never seen anything like it. Not only did he love the crystal for the way it looked, it had become his way of keeping Katherine close to him now that she was gone. Around the size of a Snicker's bar, it was coal black with a smooth, glossy finish. He could almost see his reflection when he looked into it. He would habitually handle it during his travels through the forest, rubbing his thumb against its smooth contours, a simple act that seemed to bring a strange sense of comfort. After a few moments, the heat of the crystal finally became too much, and he could no longer hold it. He hurriedly reached over and placed it on top of the wall.

He couldn't know it at the time, but that decision would change his life forever.

Chapter 6
Fireflies

As Bean placed the crystal on the wall, a piercing surge of energy radiated up his arm. He'd once received a shock from a frayed wire in his home that made his hair stand up on end and his tooth fillings hot, but there were no electrical wires out here. Mustering all his strength, he managed to unclench his fingers and free them from their grip on the rock. Shaking his hand and rubbing away the pain against his pant leg, he glimpsed, from the corner of his eye, a large tan object hurtling at him with such velocity that before he could turn fully around to identify it, he was being knocked over backward. He tumbled head over heels until he was lying flat on his back in a cloud of dust. Dazed from the blow, he opened his eyes to find himself staring straight into the razor sharp teeth of a massive mountain lion that had now perched itself heavily on his chest.

Bean squeezed his eyes shut, waiting to feel the massive fangs of the mountain lion sink into his defenseless flesh. Instead, he heard a frantic voice yelling at him, "Come on, we need to leave here! He's right behind me. We've got to go right now!"

Bean opened his eyes just in time to see the last few words emanating directly from the mouth of the mountain lion. Confused and stunned by the bewildering events of the last few seconds, he was frozen, completely unable to move.

"What's wrong with you?" the big cat shouted in a mix of a scream and roar. "If he catches us, we're done for! Done for, do you hear me?"

He continued to lie motionless, the mountain lion baring its teeth in anger. Bean could feel the heat from the panting cat's breath against his face. He felt its sharp fangs press against his neck for a moment, but, instead of biting into him, the cat chomped on the back of his collar and began to drag Bean towards the direction of the house as if he was one of its unruly cubs.

Being pulled a distance, Bean finally regained a degree of his senses and did the only thing he could do. He started to scream. And scream he did. He screamed like he never had before. The mountain lion quickly released its grip and shrieked in angry frustration, "What are you doing? The Caretaker will hear you!"

Realizing he was now free from the grasp of the mountain lion's teeth, Bean quickly scrambled to his feet and started back toward his twenty-two he'd left leaning against the wall when examining the crystal.

"Not that way," the cat screeched. "We've got to go this way," motioning with its head towards the direction of the home. The cat leapt towards Bean, grabbing his sleeve in its fangs and again began to pull him away from the wall.

Fighting as best he could in the deadly tug-of-war, Bean was no match for the powerful animal, and his legs began to buckle. Just as he was ready to submit to being dragged to what he knew was his certain death, a loud shot rang out across the field. He felt the cat's jaws loosen and, in a moment, he was free of its grip. Quickly rolling free of the animal, he turned and looked at the now lifeless body of the mountain lion at his feet, a patch of blood growing behind its front leg. Bean's head instinctively turned toward where the shot had come to see his father standing near the back door, the rifle still at his shoulder. A faint wisp of smoke rose from the end of the gun's barrel.

When Bean and his father realized the bullet had found its mark and the mountain lion was no longer a threat, they raced towards each other across the field and embraced. His father pushed him back. "Are you alright? Are you bleeding anywhere?" he said frantically, anxiously scanning Bean from head to toe looking for a wound.

"I don't think I'm hurt dad. I'm just scared. It came out of nowhere."

Satisfied that Bean was not injured, his father put his arm around him and took a deep breath, then expelled it like he was blowing out birthday candles.

"Let's get you back to the house. I think you've had enough adventure for one day."

The two were about to enter the back door of the home when Bean glanced back over his shoulder to take a final look at where the attack had taken place. Viewing the lifeless body of the mountain lion in the distance, his eyes were drawn to some movement on top of the wall. It was then Bean saw him. There, standing almost upright, its front hoofs resting on the wall, was the biggest deer he had ever seen. He gazed at the animal, quickly realizing it was no ordinary deer. Not only was the sheer size uncommon, its horns were massive and seemed to sparkle and shimmer in the morning sunlight. Although the beast was several hundred feet away, Bean could see the antlers were unusual, with each horn directed forward and the points coated in what looked like silver. The tips themselves appeared to be sharpened, making the ends like daggers. Bean shuddered thinking about what would happen to someone on the receiving end of those horns. The antlers alone were sufficiently frightening, but the creature's scarlet eyes sent a chill of terror down Bean's spine, piercing him to his very soul. They were locked onto him and he had to use all of his mental strength to break the beast's hypnotic gaze.

"Dad, look at that," he said in terrified amazement.

His father turned, Bean pointing to where the deer was standing on the wall.

"What is it son? I don't see anything." Bean again scanned the wall. The deer was gone.

"There was a huge deer out on top of the wall dad. I swear it. It was there just a second ago."

"There aren't any deer around here Bean," his father replied. "But then again, I was sure there weren't any mountain lions here either until two minutes ago. Let's get inside. You'll be safe in the house."

Entering the doorway, Bean could feel the scarlet eyes of the giant stag boring into his back. This time, he was too frightened to turn around.

Bean lay in bed, staring at the ceiling and reliving the unlikely events of the day over and over again in his mind. During the attack, his only thought was of pure survival, but as sleep's footsteps would not soon be approaching, he had time to consider the broader implications of what happened to him.

How was he was even alive? The mountain lion certainly had the tools to end him. He stared straight into the cat's mouth and witnessed up close and personal its razor-like fangs. He'd felt the long, sharp claws on his chest, but had nary a scratch on his body to show from the encounter. And it wasn't for lack of opportunity either. The mountain lion had plenty of time to do him in. It was well over a minute before Bean's father fired the deadly shot. Plenty of time for an ornery raccoon to finish him off, let alone a ferocious food chain topper.

Yes, the more he considered the matter, the clearer it became that the big cat had no intention of hurting him. As he went over what the animal had said to him, or what he had imagined it had said, it was evident its intentions were quite to the contrary. Had it actually been trying to protect him? The thought was absurd. Bean went over it again in his mind. What had it said? Something about getting away from someone. But who? The stag? Since when was a mountain lion afraid of a deer? Then again, that was no ordinary deer. When Bean closed his eyes, he could still see the red eyes of the animal. When he thought of those eyes, he felt real fear for the first time in his life.

So what to make of all of this? Voices in his head. Talking animals. It was all quite fantastic yet, strangely enough, familiar. He knew he should find the thought of speaking animals absurd, but, if he were to be honest, he had always felt it strange animals hadn't spoken to him long before now. As a young child he would often talk to the animals, fully expecting a response, and would be surprised when none came. Even when he got older and knew better, after making sure no one else was around, he would talk to the neighbor's cows like he would any other person. The cows never spoke back, but he found the one-sided conversations oddly satisfying. So it wasn't the fact the mountain lion spoke that had him puzzled.

It was that the cat was even there at all. No one he knew had ever seen a mountain lion in this forest.

Finally drifting towards an elusive sleep, he couldn't help but feel sorry his father had shot the big cat. He now wished he could speak to it and ask it where it came from and why it was here, and more importantly, what and who it was so afraid of. One shot from his father's rifle had ended any chance of that.

The last drop of consciousness slowly evaporating from his mind, he was jolted back to reality when he suddenly felt a distinct presence in the room with him. He sat up in bed scanning the darkness, expecting to see someone or something. Nothing. After fully convincing himself he was indeed alone in the room, he again rested his head on his pillow. Just as his heart rate again resumed a normal beat, his eye caught a tiny light flashing in the upper corner of the room. Although the light was small, it penetrated the darkness and forced Bean to squint slightly. He quickly realized the glow was just a harmless firefly that had made its way into the room. He loved to watch the lightning bugs in the forest during his campouts and found comfort in the soft, warm glimmer of the dancing lights above him in the trees. He thought it a good omen that one of his tiny friends had joined him in the room for the night.

After a few moments, another light flashed as a second firefly joined the first. It was unusual for one firefly to make its way into the house, let alone two. Almost before Bean could note the oddity, a third and fourth firefly appeared. He slowly rose up onto his elbows in curiosity as more and more tiny fires ignited in the corner of the room. Within less than a minute, hundreds of fireflies filled the chamber, lighting up the room as if it were mid-day. Bean's astonishment grew as the amorphous mass of sparkling fireflies slowly began to take a shape, the shape of a woman - the most beautiful woman he had ever beheld. After a moment, the woman spoke.

"Hello, Benjamin. I've missed you. I've missed you so very much."

Her voice seemed a chorus of a thousand tiny voices. It was soft, yet penetrating. He realized the woman's voice was actually the fireflies speaking to him in a unified refrain.

"I had hoped this day would never come," she said sorrowfully. "But alas, the hour is near at hand."

Bean's initial fear quickly subsided as she spoke. Her tone was comforting and he sensed the being had genuine affection for him and meant him no harm.

"You are no longer safe here. Your presence has been detected, and there is little time before they will come for you."

Bean interrupted, "Who are you? What do you want with me?"

Without replying to his queries, the woman continued.

"I am unable to come unto you in person. I have sent my friends to deliver this message. Pay heed to my words. Your life hangs in the balance."

The woman then proceeded to relate to Bean the following message, which she repeated three times:

"Benjamin, before you were, you were chosen. Your destiny and our fate have forever been one. Seek the noble and great, for your mission is not yours alone. Sacrifice is the truest sign of worthiness. Reach into the darkness, and you will seize the light. Remember, the victory of one is the ruin of many. Justice destroys only the wicked. Finally, and most importantly, remember... the end of your journey is the beginning."

Upon delivering the message for the final time, she concluded, "Now my dear Benjamin, the time is long spent. Your very destruction is at the door. Hasten to the wall. It is there you will find your escape. I pray we will be together again soon. Until then, may the Ancient of Days be with you and guide you."

With that, the light of the fireflies slowly began to wane and the image of the woman faded away into the darkness of the room. Just as the last flicker of light was extinguished, Bean heard the woman's voice whisper one final instruction; "You must take your brother with you."

Chapter 7

Maximus

The warmth of the dawning sun bathed Bean's face, returning him from the memories of the past few months to the dire reality of his current situation. He had escaped the maniacal stags for now, but he could not dispel the ominous cloud of danger he sensed was gathering on the horizon.

He looked down at the sleeping Wart, his face smashed into Bean's chest, mouth agape and emitting the occasional raspy snore. He had not been a good older brother and he knew it. In the past, he'd rationalized Wart brought it upon himself - that if not for Wart's constant teasing, he would be a kinder, gentler brother. But in that deepest place within a soul, he knew his problems with Wart started only with himself. Wart's behavior was merely a defense mechanism - a defense that was necessary because his older brother thought of him as a nuisance rather than a brother. Bean resolved to do better, just as soon as he and Wart got out of this mess.

And what a strange mess indeed. As the first glimmers of morning crept over the horizon, it became evident just how foreign Bean's new environment was. He certainly wasn't in Missouri anymore - or Kansas for that matter. Bean's world as he knew it had changed from black and white to brilliant Technicolor. If his house had not disappeared, he would surely look to see if there were any pointy witch shoes poking out from underneath it.

The leaves leaping out from the towering trees in front of him were a deep and vibrant forest green and were of such a size and vigor that they at first seemed cartoonish. On the larger trees, each leaf spanned two or three feet in large rounded fronds, with a thickness that made it seem as if he could simply walk to the top of every tree on a stairway of foliage. Some smaller trees dotted those areas where light was able to penetrate the thick canopy. Most were six or seven feet high and topped with pointed, succulent palm leaves sprouting like a shock of green hair atop the tree's rail thin trunk, forming a strange botanical army guarding the forest. Several bushes comprised of long, spiraled leaves emanating in all directions from a central base completed the distinct landscape before him. The forest floor itself was covered with a thick, lush grass nearly a foot high, each blade in perfect uniformity with its neighbor. Bean had seen pictures of the Amazon rain forest in Geography class. It had seemed so exotic and mysterious. He chuckled to himself, "the Amazon's got nothing on this place."

It wasn't long before the sun's tepid fingers pried open young Wart's eyes. Realizing he was snuggled up against his brother, he quickly sat back. The fog of sleep lifting from his mind, the events of the prior night rushed to his memory. He jumped to his feet and looked back over the wall. Disappointment and dread cascaded across his face as his nightmarish fears were confirmed. There was no home. It had not been a dream. He spun around with fire in his eyes, launching into Bean.

"This is your fault! Those crazy deer were after you! Why did you have to drag me into all this?"

"Listen Wart," Bean said in tone more earnest and kind than he had ever used with his brother. "I don't know what's going on. I'm as frightened as you are. I know you're angry with me, but we need to work together to figure this out."

"You figure it out! I'm going home," Wart said, then scrambled back over the wall and began walking across the field towards where his home used to be. Bean ran after him, grabbed him by the arm and twisted him back around.

"Warren, I know I don't deserve it, but I need you to trust me. We need to stick together."

Before Wart could spew back a response, a high, chirping, melodic voice floated across the meadow from the direction of the wall.

"When you two are finished arguing, we have business to attend to."

The boys spun around anxiously. Bean saw no one at first, but, upon scanning the scene, noticed a small sparrow perched atop the wall.

"Hasn't anyone ever told you it's not polite to stare," said the sparrow.

With that the bird left its perch on the wall and landed on the ground a few feet in front of the boys. The bird was roughly the size of a fist with small, black, lustrous eyes that reminded Bean of peering into the mouth of a cave. Its feathers were dark brown and dotted with white speckles, as if

Bean's mother had dusted it with powdered sugar like one of her famous Bundt cakes. While the bird resembled a normal sparrow in most regards, like the trees and plants around them, the brown in its feathers and the yellow in its beak were much deeper and vivid than any bird Bean had previously encountered.

"Allow me to introduce myself. My name is Maximus. Maximus DeMinimus to be more precise," the bird said appearing to bow slightly before the boys. "I have been tasked with bringing the both of you to safety. So, as I said before, if you are done arguing, we'd best be on our way."

The boys looked at each other, Wart's mouth agape in utter amazement. Bean grinned slightly. Considering himself now a seasoned pro in dealing with talking animals, he found Wart's reaction quite amusing.

He stepped forward slightly, "It's very nice to meet you Mr. DeMinimus. My name is Benjamin. This is my brother Wart... I mean Warren. If you please sir, could you tell us just exactly where we are?"

"That, my boy, is neither for me to say or for you to know," said Maximus dismissively. "Now, enough of this triviality. We have a lengthy journey ahead."

Wart blurted clumsily, "You can talk! You're a bird! You're a bird that can talk!"

Although small and black, Maximus' eyes managed to portray a look of disgust.

"Hmmm. Quite observant indeed. Yes, my boy, I can talk, which, it would seem, is more than I can say for you."

Wart, now perceiving he was being mocked, quickly lost his sense of awe at the talking bird and kicked into defense mode.

"Well at least I don't have a stupid name like Maximus DeMinimus. Your mom bird and dad bird must not have liked you very much."

"I'll have you know my good boy, and I'm being generous when I say good, that particular designation was of my own making. It is perfectly fitting to my general excellence. I am a bird for all seasons. I am all things to all things. Though I may be diminutive in nature, I assure you, I am capable of the most exquisite brilliance and accomplishment. Underestimate me, boy, at your own peril."

Sensing the escalation, Bean broke in, "Yes, I'm sure you are quite magnificent as far as talking birds go. But why should we trust you? You won't even tell us where we are or to who you're taking us."

"To whom I am taking you," Maximus corrected. "As I see it, it is not a matter of trust, but of necessity. You certainly can choose to stay here and fend for yourselves in a land filled with unknown danger and peril. I for one would choose to ally myself with someone, such as yours truly, familiar with the environs that to you, to be sure, are quite foreign. Someone who, as I do now, pledges their very life in preserving yours. I believe you have already encountered those from this land who do not seek your best interests. They will not cease in seeking you out. Do you believe if I were of that particular ilk, that we would be having the pleasant conversation we are now? In an unfamiliar land, is it not better to trust another who professes friendship, than to face the unknown alone?"

"We don't need him Bean," shot Wart. "Besides, how much help will a bird be if we run into those crazy deer again? Let's just get outta here and find our way back home."

Bean looked to the forest as if searching for an answer, then back down at Maximus. Finally, he turned to Wart and attempted to speak, but no words came.

Maximus spoke impatiently, "Yes, tough decision. What to do, what to do? One deserving of much thought and reflection indeed. But alas, time is not on our side. We must hie to the safety of the forest. It is do or die; quite literally in your case. To put it simply, I am leaving with or without you."

Bean stood silently, frozen with indecision.

"I'll take your silence as your election to stay," said Maximus irritably. "Best of luck to the both of you in your future endeavors, though, to be sure, your future and your endeavors are in great jeopardy. I'm sure it was a pleasure meeting me. I bid you a fond farewell."

With that Maximus turned and flew towards the forest. Bean looked again at Wart, this time with resolve in his eyes.

"Wait Maximus," he yelled, "we're coming with you."

Chapter 8
Always Greener

Maximus flew ahead into the forest while the boys waited. After a few minutes, he would return and inform them it was safe to move forward. This process was repeated countless times over the next few hours as the group methodically made their way into the heart of the forest.

"This part of Edinnu is not as dangerous," Maximus told the boys, "but you never can be too careful."

The small group moved along toward an abyss of both uncertainty and fascination. Bean searched for anything familiar in his surroundings, but to no avail. He attempted several times to question Maximus as to their whereabouts, but he would either ignore Bean's queries or simply state that it was not for him to say.

Wart sassed, "You sure talk a lot for someone who isn't allowed to say anything."

Maximus, unphased, replied, "I am allowed to say anything I wish, young man. However, there are times when wisdom dictates discretion. And you, my boy, have made it abundantly clear in our brief time together, that there is a considerable lack of discretion in what passes from your lips, with which I can only infer to mean there is a corresponding lack of wisdom."

Bean rather enjoyed the feisty exchanges between Wart and Maximus. It seemed to him the two were made for each other and he liked that Wart had finally met his match. He also welcomed the brief respite from being the main focus of Wart's anger and venom.

The sun now at its zenith, the group arrived at a clearing bursting with long lush grass.

"Wait here," said Maximus as he again flew ahead to scout the area.

Bean and Wart surveyed the field from the cover of the forest. A path bordered by a wooden fence cut the clearing into what appeared to be two equal halves. On one side of the fence was a cow grazing lazily in the meadow. The grass was so vivid and luscious that Bean felt a twinge of jealousy towards the cow as it munched away. Either that or his stomach was reminding him he hadn't yet eaten that day. The cow was a shimmering black except for a patch of white extending from the top of its head to the tip of its nose, as if someone had taken a paintbrush slathered with white paint and made a bold strike down the cow's forehead.

Wart looked at Bean impatiently, "I'm tired of waiting for that stupid bird. There's nothing out there but a cow. I'm going."

With that, Wart bolted into the open field. Bean reached to grab him but was too late.

"Wait Wart," he exclaimed. "It's not safe. Get back here!"

Wart, never one to heed his older brother's pleas even in the best of circumstances, proceeded without hesitation, leaving Bean no choice but to follow him out into the clearing. It wasn't long before the lone cow took notice of the approaching boys. It hurriedly moved towards a small gate in the middle of the fence.

"Excuuse mmme lads. I say, excuuse mmme lads," the cow said in a slow, low, baritone voice.

Bean was quite pleased upon hearing the cow speak. It was just how he'd imagined the neighbor cows would have sounded if they had have ever spoken back to him. The boys made their way to the gate where the cow was standing.

"Goood lads, goood lads," the cow warbled. "Wooould you be so kind as tooo open this gate so that I mmmay pass throoough? I have been admmmiring the grass on the other side of this fence for quite sommme timmme now. It is clearly of a quality far superior tooo the grass on this side. I can scarcely stommmach this rotten crabgrass I'm forced tooo eat when such a delicacy lay only a few feet out of mmmmy reach."

The boys looked at each other and then at the grass, first on the cow's side of the fence and then on their own. Neither could identify any discernible difference between the grasses on either side.

Bean spoke, "I'm sorry, we can't open the gate. I don't want your owner to get upset if you get out."

A look of disgust crossed the cow's face.

"Nooo one owns mmme!" it said with disdain. "Now open this gate without any further delay and I'll forgive yooou your immmpuuudence."

Maximus darted back towards the boys, clearly upset.

"What part of wait here did you not understand?"

Not waiting for a response, he continued, "For future reference, the word 'wait' means to remain, stay, linger or loiter. The word 'here' references the site, location, place, position, setting, scene, locality, whereabouts or spot where I left you previously and instructed you with the aforementioned command to wait. Perhaps I have given you boys too much credit by assuming you could understand the most basic of directions."

Wart piped up, "It's not that we don't understand you, it's that we DON'T CARE! And for future reference, 'care' means the thing that we don't do whenever you say anything."

Maximus replied tersely, "Well you'd better start caring and quick. You have no idea the danger you are in. My words, which you so cavalierly disregard, may be the last things that you don't care about."

"If yooou don't mmmind. Could yooou please be so kind as to take a brief hiatus frommm your arguuummment and open the gate?" interjected the cow.

"Alright, alright," Wart snapped, "if it will shut you up."

He took a few steps and unhooked the latch to the gate. The cow almost trampled Wart in its eagerness to get to the heretofore forbidden grass. The gate swung back with a bang as the latch once again secured itself firmly against the fence post.

"Goood lad, goood lad," moaned the cow, ecstasy salivating off its words as it eagerly dipped its head into the grass and began grazing voraciously.

As much as he enjoyed the tête-à-tête between Wart and Maximus, Bean was more keen than Wart to the dangers Maximus described. He had looked into the eyes of the stag one too many times to not know that a very real evil was after them. He jumped in before Wart and Maximus could resume their argument.

"Listen Wart, I know you're scared. I'm scared too. I know you want to get back to Mom and Dad. I do too. I can't explain where we are or why we're here, I only know that so far, Maximus is our only friend. I don't know how I know, but I truly believe he is on our side. You don't need to like him, but for now, we need to listen to him. If you can't trust him, I'm asking you to trust me."

"First of all, I'm not scared," said Wart defiantly. "Second of all, I'm not as convinced as you are that this bird is our friend. I'll trust you for now Bean, but the bird's got to do something more than boss us around if he expects us to follow him around like little hatchlings. He needs to answer a few questions before we take another step."

"Pardon mmme," said the cow. "Upon further reflection, it appears that the grass on this side of the fence was not as it first appeared. It is clear to mmme now that the grass on the other side of the fence is of a mmmuch superior quality. Would yooou be so kind as tooo open the gate again so I mmmay pass back tooo the other side?"

Bean and Wart looked at each other with a silent you've got to be kidding me, but it was Maximus that spoke.

"Listen cow, we are not here to be your personal doormen. The grass is quite the same on either side. Kindly leave us be."

"I prommmise not tooo bother yooou again if yooou let mmme throoough the gate just once mmmore," pleaded the cow.

Bean, figuring there could be no harm in letting the cow back into the area where they had first encountered him, stepped to the gate and again unlatched it. Once more, the cow rushed through the opening and quickly stuffed its nose into the green grass on the other side.

"You are a truuue gentlemmman, a truuue gentlemmman indeed," mumbled the cow through a mouthful of grass.

"So what's it gonna be Maximus? Are you going to come clean or are we done here?" queried Wart matter-of-factly.

Maximus alit on the fence post nearest the boys, pausing as if deciding how best to proceed. After a few moments, he spoke with a sincerity of which the boys were unfamiliar.

"It is not my intent to keep you in the dark. Believe me when I say, your safety is of paramount concern both to me and to those that sent me. I am silent only because any information I give you may bring danger to both you and those from whence I came and of whom I am a part. With that said, I agree to answer what I can. What do you want to know?"

Chapter 9
Seven Hunter

The day before Katherine vanished, she took Bean to the large maple tree down the lane from their home. Sitting with their backs against the base of the trunk, they enjoyed the cool spring breeze. As she had done so many times before, she began singing his favorite song about a magical lollipop tree.

One fine day in early spring I played a funny trick
Right in the yard behind our house I planted a lollipop stick
Then every day I watered it well and watched it carefully
I hoped one day that stick would grow to be a lollipop tree

Ha ha-ha, Ho-ho-ho
What a sight to see
Me and my lollipop, lollipop, lollipop, lolli-lolli-lollipop tree

Then one day I woke to find a very lovely sight
A tree all full of lollipops had grown in the dark of the night

I sat beneath that wonderful tree and looked up with a grin
And when I opened up my mouth a pop would drop right in

Ha-ha-ha, Oh-ho-ho
What a place to be
Under a lollipop, lollipop, lollipop lolli-lolli-lollipop tree

Winter came and days grew cold as winter days will do
On my tree my lovely tree not one little lollipop grew
From every branch an icicle hung, the twigs were bare as bones
But when I broke the icicles off they turned to ice cream cones

Ha-ha-ha, Oh-ho-ho
How I danced with glee
Under the lollipop, lollipop, lollipop, lolli-lolli-lollipop tree

Even though Bean knew the song by heart, it would always make him sad when the winter came and there were no more lollipops growing on the tree. Sadness would quickly give way to pure delight when the boy in the song broke an icicle off and it turned into an ice cream cone.

Bean treasured the times when it was just him and Katherine. She was unfailingly kind to him. It was never a chore for her to babysit, and she always seemed genuinely happy to spend time with him. She was an oasis of kindness and friendship in a desert of indifference and loneliness. Of course, Bean's parents were always supportive and loving, but it was different with Katherine. She was under no parental obligation to like him, but somehow, she did.

Though he made it his general practice to keep his feelings for anyone or anything well hidden, as she finished the song, he snuggled up against her arm and quietly murmured, "I love you, Sissy."

Katherine sat him up and turned him so she was staring directly and intently into his eyes.

"I love you too. I want you to know that you are very special to me. I will always be there for you."

But she wasn't. The next day she was gone, and with her, his only friend.

He went back to the old maple a few times after Katherine's disappearance, searching for even the smallest degree of comfort. Sitting against the trunk, he would softly sing the lollipop tree song, but there was no longer any joy in it. When Katherine was with him, the thought of lollipop trees didn't seem so fantastic. He would gaze up, imagining himself plucking a tasty treat off the branches. When she vanished, all of the magic in Bean's world disappeared with her.

Bean hadn't thought of the lollipop tree in years, but, as he walked through this strange new land, he found himself humming the song. It wouldn't have surprised him in the least if he turned the corner and ran smack dab into a genuine lollipop tree. The uncertainty of his situation brought great fear and anxiety to be sure, but he had not been happier since that last day with Katherine under the maple tree. He felt at home.

⧫⧫⧫

In unison, Bean and Wart blurted out the first question to Maximus, "Where are we?"

"This land is called Edinnu. It is the land of our father, the Ancient of Days. It has been from the beginning and will be until it is finished."

"Why are crazy deer trying to kill us?" exclaimed Wart.

"Ah yes, the Caretakers. A nasty bunch those. Best not to get on the bad side of that lot. Too late for you two though, I suppose. The Caretakers are the personal guard for One. They are bound under an ancient dark alliance between their ancestors and the ancestors of One. Their evil knows no limits and their cruelty no bounds."

"Well that's just super, Maximus. I feel much better now. And what did we do to make these rays of sunshine so upset?"

"It was nothing you did my little man," replied Maximus. "It was what your brother did. Or rather, who your brother is."

Wart glanced at Bean with a look of disdain, as if to say he knew all along that this whole mess was his fault.

"And just who is my brother?" Wart asked.

"Your brother is the Deliverer," replied Maximus matter-of-factly.

"Listen birdbrain, don't be stingy with the information. The deliverer of what?"

"Not of what, but of whom. He will deliver us all, even you my dear Warren."

"Excuuuse mmme gentlemmmen. I hate to be a bother, but would yooou be so kind as tooo..."

Before the cow could finish its sentence, Wart stomped over to the gate, swung it open, and kicked it so hard it broke off its hinges.

"There you go you stupid cow. No more gate. Knock yourself out," Wart yelled.

"What have yooou done?" moaned the cow in terror. "I ammm undone. I ammm undone. Yooou have destroyed the gate. I ammm undone."

Wart was taken aback at the reaction of the cow.

"Geesh, don't have a man, cow."

Wart was the only one that chuckled at his little joke. Bean noted that, for the first time, the cow was no longer focused on eating the grass. Rather, it continued its histrionics, lamenting the fact that Wart had broken the gate.

Bean walked over to the cow and put his hand on its neck in an effort to comfort the animal.

"There, there. It will be okay. It's just a fence."

"I'm afraid it will be anything but okay for him," said Maximus. "Warren's little temper tantrum has undoubtedly signed this animal's death warrant. One does not tolerate any destruction of property, or any disobedience for that matter. Particularly not from an ani..."

Maximus stopped mid-sentence, cocking his head upward as if straining to see or hear something that wasn't there. He tilted his head back to the other side. The boys looked at him waiting for him to continue, but only the sound of the cow's wailing broke the silence.

Finally, Maximus slowly whispered, "We need to leave now." Louder and more forcefully, he repeated, "We need to leave right now! Follow me!" Maximus darted towards the tree line. Bean and Wart looked at each other for a moment, then, in unison, began running frantically after Maximus, away from some unseen danger.

Bean broke through the forest line at the point Maximus entered and continued running through the dense foliage. Due to Wart's rotund shape and general aversion to physical exercise, he wasn't the runner Bean was and, after about a hundred yards, Bean realized Wart was no longer behind him. He stopped running and turned, looking for his brother. He could see no one. He turned back looking for Maximus. Again, no one.

Angry at himself for not staying with Wart, knives of panic stabbed at him. Yelling for his brother, he ran back the way he had come. He had taken only a few steps when suddenly his feet were swept out from under him and he found himself looking up through the trees at the clear sky. In an instant, he felt a weight on his chest and the cold steel of a knife blade pressing against his throat. Then, into his view, appeared the visage of a young girl. She brought her face within inches of his and carefully examined his every feature. Her penetrating stare seemed to paralyze him, that and the blade at his throat that was now beginning to draw a trickle of blood.

She moved her face slowly along his neck, her breath warming his skin while sending a shiver down his spine. She took a deep breath, as if taking a long sniff of his scent. For a brief, awkward moment, he wished he had taken a shower back at home the day before, but the pain in his neck soon snapped him out of the trivial insecurities of a teenage boy into the dire reality of his current situation.

He attempted to speak, but just as he opened his mouth, the girl gently placed a finger against his lips. She again brought her head toward Bean and, for a moment, it seemed she was about to kiss him, her lips parting ever so slightly. His heart began racing even faster than it already was, threatening now to leap out of his chest. But the girl's mouth stopped just an inch from his, traveled across his cheek to his ear where she whispered almost imperceptibly, "Shhhhh. You must remain still."

Her soft breath tickled his ear, making it almost impossible to comply with her instructions, yet somehow he managed to lie there, motionless.

Minutes passed, minutes that seemed to stretch into an eternity. The pressure of the knife blade had long been eased, but the close proximity to someone of the opposite sex (someone that wasn't his mother or sister that is), caused Bean an entirely different kind of discomfort, one which to him was entirely unfamiliar. The girl laid her body on top of his as if to shield him from someone or something; her face remaining just inches above his. She continued to scan his every feature as if looking for something. Given her proximity, he was helpless to avoid looking at her as well. He felt short of breath, not because of the weight of the girl, which couldn't have been more than 80 or 90 pounds, but because he found himself literally inches from the prettiest girl he had ever seen.

Finally, Bean heard the sound of a chirping bird to his left, and shortly thereafter, one from his right. The girl lifted herself slightly and brought her lips together. Again, Bean thought – hoped - he might be about to receive a kiss. Instead, a whistle mimicking some sort of bird flew out of her mouth. He marveled that such a sound could come from the lips of a human - at least he assumed she was human.

"You're safe now," she whispered as she took away the knife from his neck and tenderly dabbed at the dried blood with a cloth she pulled from her pocket. "I am sorry about that. I had to be sure you didn't make a sound. I must go."

She raised herself off his body and sheathed her knife into a leather pouch strapped to her forearm. As she stood, Bean was able to take in the full measure of the girl for the first time. Appearing sixteen or seventeen, her lustrous black hair was pulled back tightly into a pony tail that reached the middle of her back. The eyes with which he had become intimately familiar in their few minutes together were a hazel green with dapples of blue that made it seem as if he was looking across the lake near his home when the last rays of sun reflected across the water's surface at dusk. She couldn't have been more than five feet tall, with no muscle to speak of. He wondered how someone so small could have tackled him with such great force. She wore a kind of leather pullover, reminiscent of the outfits the squaws wore in the old cowboy and indian movies his dad liked to watch. In addition to the knife on her wrist, she had a kind of mechanical armament spanning her opposite forearm, commencing at her elbow and ending in a leather strap between her thumb and her index finger. A conical sheath was affixed on her back, just below her neck, that appeared to contain small, arrow-like missiles. Her weaponry was completed with a long knife strapped to her right calf.

The girl turned to leave. Bean reached up impulsively and grabbed her by the hand.

"Wait, what is your name," he asked urgently.

She turned back to him and smiled ever so slightly.

"My name is Seven Hunter."

With that she vanished into the wilderness.

Chapter 10
Mahan

Several hours had passed since Bean's encounter with the girl. He had wandered in the forest for much of that time attempting to locate Wart and Maximus, but to no avail. He tried to make his way back to the clearing where the group encountered the fickle cow, but he'd lost all bearings when knocked to the ground by - what did she say her name was? Ah yes, Hunter, Seven Hunter. An odd name to say the least. Of course, he couldn't cast any stones when it came to names. He figured Seven was likely a nickname. She probably had a meddlesome little sister that came up with that one. Then again, this place was beyond strange and it would be no surprise to him if the names of the inhabitants were equally bizarre.

With the setting of the sun, he found himself alone in the dark. He had spent many nights alone in the forest by his home and actually preferred sleeping on the ground to his comfortable bed. But this was very different. The unfamiliar surroundings, combined with the traumatic events of the last twenty-four hours, had thrown his mind into a fragile and precarious state. Adding to his woes, with the darkness crept a certain feeling of vertigo. He lay on the soft grassy forest floor, trying to reorient himself by gazing up at the stars as he did back home. Before long, the demands of the day exacted their toll and, as he slowly drifted off to sleep, he felt as if he was floating aimlessly through space.

He awoke with a start, not due to any particular noise, but to the distinct presence of someone or something nearby. The moon had risen since Bean had fallen asleep, and he could now discern the outline of the forest bathed in the soft dreamlike glow of the moonlight. He rose to his feet, trying to identify the intrusion.

He whispered loudly into the darkness, "Wart? Maximus? Who's there?" No answer.

Peering into the night, he walked forward carefully, soon coming to a slightly worn path through the trees. He looked down the pathway in one direction, and then the other. Turning to look again in the first direction, it occurred to him something was now amiss. He strained his neck forward in an effort to make out a dark shape 100 yards down the path. It appeared to be the form of a man, a very large man, but he remained motionless. It was impossible to make out any features in the distance, only a dark, hulking silhouette. Bean's first instinct was to run, but curiosity fastened him to his spot. Curiosity and the slim hope that he may have stumbled upon someone who might be able to help him out of his current predicament.

He could not see the being's eyes, but Bean could feel the heavy weight of its stare upon him. Any hope this creature would be of help quickly dispersed into the blackness of the night. An overwhelming feeling of dread swept over Bean, and he determined it in his best interest to leave and to leave quickly, but, as he turned to run, he discovered his legs to be utterly uncooperative. Struggling to free himself, an invisible force began pressing down upon his shoulders until, unable to stand any longer, he fell helplessly to his hands and knees. He had never encountered such a complete and utter darkness. Like a massive wave crashing upon him, it overwhelmed his helpless body, tossing his spirit to and fro. His stomach lurched violently and it was all he could do not to be sick on himself. Gloom and sadness shrouded his mind with such intensity that, for a moment, he wished himself dead, if only to gain a reprieve from the oppressing weight of evil that now rested squarely upon him.

Managing to raise his head and reach out his arm toward the being, he cried feebly, "Please... help me."

His voice roused the creature, and it slowly began to move down the path toward him. As it approached, Bean realized he had underestimated its size. It was not simply large; it was massive, at least eight feet tall and well over 400 pounds. While it looked hooded from a distance, as it approached, he could see it was instead the creature's long hair draping over its shoulders and running down to its chest. Several strands of hair hung over its face, hiding whatever features the moonlight might have revealed to Bean.

The beastly man stopped a few feet in front of him. It slowly bent over and reached down with its giant hand, grabbing Bean by the throat. Its fingers felt cold and ashy against Bean's neck. It slowly lifted Bean off his knees and onto his feet, then on to his tiptoes. Instinctively grabbing its forearms, Bean was lifted off the ground and raised high in the air so he was now looking straight into the face of the creature.

He managed to somehow whisper through the tight grip squeezing his neck, "Please... don't."

Seemingly unaffected by Bean's pleas, the creature methodically lifted its other hand and brushed back the long, entangled strands of hair from its face. Bean was now able to gaze into its ghastly visage for the first time. It was black, but that wasn't the color of its skin. It seemed to Bean its entire body was bathed in soot, which had somehow infused itself with the skin of the creature. The beast brought Bean to within just a few inches of its face. Its breath was hot with an acrid smell of rotting flesh and Bean was helpless to avoid it washing into his nostrils. The being moved Bean in the air like a rag doll, slowly examining every inch of his face. Finally, it brought him almost nose to nose.

Their eyes met. Bean's stomach dropped as if descending the first big hill of a roller coaster. The fiend exuded the most profound grief and despair, while at the same time, was utterly devoid of any type of human emotion. Bean felt as if he was peering into the very eyes of death itself. He wished he could be buried under the highest mountain rather than endure the gaze any longer. Summoning every ounce of determination in his soul, he was finally able to break the creature's hypnotic stare. He looked down at the beast's bare bosom, noticing it was covered in a thick matted hair, almost like fur. The distraction provided a brief but welcome break from the oppressive darkness that clouded his mind.

"Who are you?" Bean rasped.

The giant man turned him slightly so its putrefied mouth pressed against Bean's ear and whispered slowly, in a voice like far off thunder, "I am Ruin. I am Despair. I am Devastation. I am Murder. I am Master - I am MAHAN."

The creature opened its mouth so Bean was looking straight into its throat. Bean heard a crackling, snapping sound in each ear and realized it was the sound of the creature's jaw slowly breaking, its mouth opening wider and wider to the point where it completely enveloped Bean's head. He was now seeing directly into the gullet of the beast, and it occurred to him he was about to be swallowed whole, like a mouse being eaten by a snake. He could feel the hot saliva on his skin and the roughness of the beast's tongue as his head squeezed into its mouth. He strangely felt no panic now, only resignation as his fate was sealed. Death would be a welcome friend. Slowly descending down the creature's throat, Bean opened his eyes only to see a blackness that surpassed all description. Finally, as he was drifting into a last sleep, he could make out a soft glowing light in the distance, like the last few embers of a dying fire. He could no longer feel the restrictions of the creature's throat pressing against his body.

It now seemed as if he was flying through the darkness, moving nearer to the distant fire. As he drew closer, he detected a low murmur coming from the direction of a horizon now ablaze with massive firestorms. The noise increasing, his last glimmer of hope extinguished as he realized the sounds were the shrieks of thousands of damned souls, writhing and moaning with cries of utter anguish and despair. He now knew exactly who the creature was. It was Hell itself. Bean closed his eyes and drifted away into nothingness.

Chapter II
Captured

Bean sat up with a jolt, gasping for breath. Quickly glancing around for any sign of the creature, he was greatly relieved to find himself alone in what appeared to be the exact location where he had fallen asleep the night before. Trying to convince himself his nightmare was just that - a dream - his best efforts could not erase the palpable feeling of despair that still clung to his soul like the dew on the grass underneath him.

"I'm glad you're awake," came a voice from above. "We've a long day ahead of us."

Already in a fragile state, Bean jerked around violently, ready for a fight, scanning the trees for the source of the voice. There, perched innocently on a neighboring branch, was Maximus.

"Where have you been?" screamed Bean in anger and relief.

"Now, now, my boy. Just calm down," said Maximus reassuringly. "It is with sincere regret that I inform you, in the hustle and bustle of yesterday's ill-fated circumstances, Wart was... well, captured. It was necessary I follow him to ascertain the location of his incarceration. With that accomplished, I have returned to you post haste. It was never my intention to leave --"

"Captured!" Bean screamed in horror.

The thought of little Wart being taken unleashed a flood of fear and emotion he hadn't felt sense Katherine disappeared.

A sudden realization shook him, "Not by the..." he couldn't bring himself to say it.

"No, no, not by the Caretakers, that would be an entirely different story, indeed," said Maximus, trying to sound soothing. "No, we had the unfortunate happenstance of running directly into a hunting party from Seven City. Mistook you and your brother for a couple of poachers I should think. Wart isn't the swiftest of foot is he? I'm afraid he was easy pickings for the hunters. It's lucky they didn't shoot him with their armbows, I suppose. But, I see you managed to avoid capture," Maximus stated with both a hint of surprise and respect.

Bean thought it best to keep his capture by the young girl to himself, in an effort to retain both this new found admiration from Maximus, as well as to avoid sharing what may be sensitive information with someone he did not yet fully trust.

"Yeah, guess I got lucky. Now, where have they taken Wart? We need to leave right now. We've got to save him!" Bean urged, panicked.

"In good time, in good time," replied Maximus. "We just can't run off willy nilly. And must I remind you we wouldn't be in this spot to begin with if you boys had paid me better heed. Rest assured, we will save your brother, but we must be prudent. Both of you in prison will help no one."

"All right, all right," Bean snipped impatiently. "Just tell me where they've taken him? I presume you have a plan, so let's hear it?"

"Quite right, my boy, quite right," chirped Maximus. "The hunters have taken Wart to Seven City. It is the outermost of the seven cities that comprise the Grand Order, agrarian in nature, comprised mostly of hunters and farmers. Not much of a prison to speak of really. Shouldn't be much trouble freeing Wart, but we have to act quickly. It won't be long before he is transferred to One City and getting him out of prison there will be considerably more problematic indeed. For now, it does not appear Wart's captors are aware of his true identity. A detail that is very much in our favor. Likely won't be much of a guard I'm guessing. I was able to get close enough to speak to Wart on his journey to Seven City, and I directed him in no uncertain terms that he was not to speak, but we both know how well Wart takes direction. Even if he doesn't talk, if he is delivered to One City, it will not be long before they get it out of him by one means or another. Once it is known you and your brother are in Edinnu, the game will change dramatically for all of us."

"But, don't they already know we're here?" queried Bean. "Surely the Caretaker that attacked us told them we made it over the wall."

"Ah yes... about that," pondered Maximus. "That particular Caretaker still remains in your land. When you crossed over the wall, you grabbed the key stone, did you not? Well of course you did, otherwise you would be deer food instead of standing here with me."

"I don't know anything about a key stone. The deer just disappeared and we ended up in this place," replied Bean.

"And you didn't do anything significant before the Caretaker vanished?" Maximus questioned leadingly.

"No, I just grabbed the crystal and..." Bean paused with a sudden look of realization. "You mean this is the key stone?" he asked pulling the black object from his pocket and holding it out in his palm.

Maximus recoiled a few feet before slowly approaching the crystal in Bean's hands. He hovered around the rock, examining it with great awe and interest.

"I've heard much of them, but have never actually seen one."

"It's just my sister's rock," offered Bean meekly.

"That's where you are wrong my boy. That rock, as you call it, is how you came to be in this place. It is the mechanism by which a door is opened between our worlds. It is how the ancients first came from your world back into Edinnu after the expulsion."

"But how did my sister get it?"

"I'm sure I do not know exactly, but I suspect she found it when you were delivered to your adoptive parents. It was sent with you so that, at some point in the future, you could return if necessary. It was thought at the time there were only two key stones remaining. The second stone was destroyed when those that delivered you came again to this land. Its destruction was necessary to ensure One would not be able to possess it and use it to get to you. Of course, we weren't expecting you to do the job for him. But that is water under the bridge as they say, no? The important thing for you to know now is many died to acquire and protect that stone. And, if you ever wish to return again to your home, I suggest you do everything in your power to keep it safe."

"No, no it doesn't work. I put it back on the wall after we crossed over, and nothing happened," Bean replied in frustration.

"That's because you used it at the exit. You need to use it at the entrance of course."

"And where is the entrance?" asked Bean with a tone of both confusion and irritation.

"All in good time, my boy," replied Maximus. "You are not going anywhere unless we rescue your brother. We have a long journey ahead and we must be off."

As Bean began the journey to Seven City, his mind raced with the new information bombarding his mind. Wart's capture, key stones, Caretakers - it was almost too much to take in. His heart ached for his parents for the first time since his arrival. He knew everything would be all right if they were here, even if they were his adopted parents. Then, suddenly, Maximus' words dawned on him. He was brought from this land to his home in Missouri. He was adopted. That could mean only one thing. His real parents must be from Edinnu.

Bean screamed excitedly, "Maximus, Maximus, wait! Are my parents here? Are they alive?"

Bean had never allowed himself to think too much about his birth parents. After all, if they didn't want him, he didn't want them either. However, with this new revelation, a flood of questions and emotions swept over him. Maximus wasn't much help. He refused to answer any questions about Bean's mother and father, saying it wasn't for him to say, and that Bean should focus on the task at hand. Clearly Maximus had much more information regarding the matter, but Bean decided not to press him, figuring there would be plenty of time to interrogate his feathered friend after he had accomplished his first and most important mission, saving Wart.

The duo traveled most of the day in the same manner as they had previously, Maximus scouting ahead some distance while Bean waited until word that the coast was clear. They would then travel a few hundred yards together. He lost track of the number of times they repeated the process, stopping only a few times to drink from a stream or eat berries or fruits from the many plants and bushes along the way. Each plant seemed to be overburdened with a delectable bounty, most of it resembling something he had eaten in his world, but as he bit into each piece, an explosion of taste and flavor almost overwhelmed his taste buds. It seemed to him he was just now tasting food for the first time. At least, he thought, I don't have to worry about starving to death in this place.

Waiting for Maximus to return from his scout, Bean would sit at the base of a tree and ponder the events of the past few months. Inevitably, his mind would settle upon the night when he was visited by the woman made of fireflies. Was this his mother? She was so magnificent. Closing his eyes, he could still see her face in his mind, as if the light from the fireflies had permanently burned her image into his corneas. He usually wasn't very good at memorizing things, but what she'd told him came to his mind clearly and easily. He repeated her words over and over:

"Benjamin, before you were, you were chosen. Your destiny and our fate have forever been one. Seek the noble and great, for your mission is not yours alone. Sacrifice is the truest sign of worthiness. Reach into the darkness, and you will seize the light. Remember, the victory of one is the ruin of many. Justice destroys only the wicked. Finally, and most importantly, remember... the end of your journey is the beginning."

His mind raced to decipher the meaning of it all? "She said she missed me," he muttered to himself. He was sure he would remember if he'd ever seen her before. How could she miss me if she had never met me? Finally, he resolved within himself that the nighttime visitor was, in fact, his mother. After all, what other explanation could there be?

Contemplating the now distinct possibility that his parents were somewhere in this strange land, a feeling of agitation suddenly set upon his mind. He sat up erect, listening intently for any danger. He heard nothing. Finally, it dawned on him - he really did hear nothing. There was no sound, only a perfect quiet. No birds, insects, animals... nothing. In fact, now that he heard it, the silence was almost deafening. He was upset with himself for not perceiving the nothingness before. For someone that spent so much time in the forest, he should have picked up on it sooner.

But what did it mean? Perhaps there weren't any animals in Edinnu. He quickly dispelled that notion, after all, his traveling companion was a bird, and they did have that most unfortunate encounter with the cow the day before. And insects? He realized he hadn't seen any of those either. But the womanly apparition in his room said she sent her firefly friends to give him the message. Surely they came from Edinnu. Maybe, he thought, animals and insects just don't make noises here. After all, if the animals can talk, maybe they have no need to make the sounds he had become accustomed to in his world.

When Maximus returned, Bean asked eagerly, "So what's with the quiet? Where are all the animals and bugs?"

"So you noticed, my boy. Your observational capacities continue to impress. Yes, we have now entered what some call the dead zone. Not as ominous as it sounds I suppose. You see, we are quickly approaching Seven City. Those animals that are one with the True Believers have long since fled to the east to join their brothers and sisters. As for the non-believers, I'm sad to say the hunters have taken care of most of them, save the few that managed to escape to the western lands. I'm afraid the growing population of the Grand Order has further depleted any remaining faunae. Not long ago, there was little demand for meat, and killing animals was prohibited. Sadly, circumstances changed dramatically with the reign of One's father, and One's rule has only compounded the problem. The hunting party we encountered was no doubt on its way to the western lands to search for game. I'm guessing Wart was their biggest catch in months. Of course, there are those animals that have joined the Grand Order, but only those that are of a particular use to One are permitted to live with the human population. You've met the Caretakers. As for what you call bugs, we don't have many of those here in Edinnu. Mostly butterflies, fireflies, bees and such."

"But that is neither here nor there, my boy. We've matters far more pressing that we must concern ourselves with. We are not far from Seven City now. I've arranged for some more appropriate attire for you. I'm afraid your current wardrobe is not much of a disguise," Maximus said with a touch of disgust.

Bean looked down at his clothes. He hadn't had much reason to think about them until now. Heat or cold had not been a concern for him in this place. Even at night, the temperature seemed perfectly moderate and pleasant.

Maximus flittered past his right ear and alit upon his shoulder.

"Just up ahead there, in the hollow of that tree," directed Maximus pointing with the tip of his wing. "And don't forget to remove your shoes."

Arriving at the tree he found a brown leather-like pullover secreted in a small hole at its base. The clothing looked very similar to what Seven Hunter was wearing in their brief encounter. Heeding Maximus' direction, he quickly removed his shoes and socks. He was accustomed to not wearing shoes in the summer so his feet were sufficiently toughened, but even the softest of feet wouldn't have much trouble in Edinnu. The grass blanketing the forest floor was something akin to the finest shag carpet one could buy, and there wasn't a thorn or briar to be found in all the land as far as Bean could tell.

He dressed in the outfit, depositing his clothes and shoes in the tree. Stretching out his arms, he discovered he enjoyed the newfound freedom the change afforded him. He had always felt restricted in the shirts and pants his mother bought him, and not only because they rarely fit. In fact, he had acquired quite a reputation in his family for being an exhibitionist, preferring to wear only his underwear when he could get away with it.

Maximus walked across his shoulders and nestled in the hood that hung off the collar of the pullover, concealing himself amongst the leather and a substantial amount of Bean's thick brown hair. Bean always wore his hair longer than his mother liked and rarely, if ever, made any attempt to style it, thereby making it a fitting nest for Maximus to hide in.

"Now listen and listen well my boy," said Maximus in a suddenly serious tone. "We are very near to Seven City. Although it is the outermost city in the Grand Order, it is not devoid of danger and peril. I will guide you to safety. If you are stopped or anything untoward happens, just do as I say and all will be well. So what say you, are you up for the challenge?" queried Maximus.

Bean didn't answer. He simply turned and began walking determinedly towards the outskirts of Seven City.

Chapter 12
Seven City

During one of the brief rests on their journey, Maximus informed Bean Seven City was part of an autocratic society called the Grand Order. It was the outermost city in the Grand Order, which itself was comprised of, as you might expect, seven cities in total. One City was the central city and the head of government. Fittingly, it was in One City where One resided. Despite Bean's many inquiries, Maximus would not go into much detail about One, other than to say he was the despotic ruler of the Grand Order, and his ruthlessness and malevolence were of a depth and profundity that was unmatched in the history of Edinnu. As with most of the words that came out of Maximus' mouth, Bean wasn't quite sure what profundity meant, but he was certain it wasn't good.

Each city was given a number designation in accordance with its proximity to One City, hence, Seven City was the farthest away of the cities. Maximus said the cities were not given a name, other than a numerical designation, so as to discourage any feelings of pride or independence in the inhabitants of that particular city. Each was to be a part of the Grand Order collective. Like limbs on the body, each performed the functions of its particular sphere, but inseparable from, and meant exclusively to benefit, the whole. Or as Maximus corrected himself, to benefit the head - One.

Maximus secreted himself in his hiding spot behind Bean's neck as the two approached the large swaths of farmland that had been cut out of the forest, forming a large agricultural moat surrounding the City. He instructed Bean to avoid looking anyone in the eye, nor was he to speak to anyone they encountered. If spoken to, he was to repeat verbatim only what Maximus whispered in his ear.

As Bean encountered the first dwellings, it struck him immediately they were virtually identical in every respect. Each home was perfectly square, 20 feet on each side, and made of what appeared to be a type of mud brick that gave the homes a tannish hue. The rooftops were made of wooden beams tightly interlaced with long fronds from some of the native vegetation he recognized from his journey through the forest. While each home stood alone, only a shoulder width gap separated the outer wall of one home from another. There were no windows and only one door that faced outward toward the main dirt road. Each home had two sets of large block numbers painted to the right of the door, separated by a dash. The first number appeared to be sequential and grew smaller as Bean walked deeper and deeper into the heart of the City.

The blocks were as uniform as the homes, each a perfect square with ten to fifteen homes along each side. In the center of each section was one larger building that Bean guessed was some sort of common hall for the residents of that particular block. Walking along, he noted the streets were conspicuously empty. He only encountered a handful of people on his entire journey, and none of them seemed particularly interested in him, not even glancing in his direction as he walked by.

Just as Bean began to think rescuing Wart may not prove to be that difficult a task after all, a loud bell began ringing from the direction he was walking. Immediately, the doors of the homes swung open and people began to pour into the streets. Soon Bean was swept up in a wave of citizenry carrying him towards the center of the City.

Maximus whispered into his ear reassuringly, "Just walk along with them; they are going precisely where we need to be."

The mass of people moved onward, plodding in uncomfortable silence. No greetings, no small talk, just the sound of hundreds of feet shuffling along the dirt road. Bean worried that, in the quiet, someone might hear Maximus' whisperings, but it was clear if any one did hear, they didn't care.

As the group neared the City center, the streets became more and more crowded until Bean was walking shoulder to shoulder with the others in the throng. Finally, the mass of people bottle-necked at a metal gate that fed into a large public square - the heart of Seven City. Several sizable, ornate buildings lined the inner perimeter of the square, a stark contrast to the scores of humbly identical homes that comprised the rest of the City. In the middle of the square was a massive black obelisk, about fifty feet high. On top was perched a giant statue of a man, his hand outstretched downward as if reaching out to the gathering of people now encircling the figure below. Carved in large letters into the marble pedestal at the base of the obelisk were the words: "ALL GLORY TO ONE."

Just as the last of the people collected into the square, another loud bell pierced the air. Maximus whispered, "Do as the others do."

The group now turned in unison to face the statue. The bell rang again and the masses dropped to their knees in perfect synchronization. Bean was a bit behind the group in kneeling, but again, no one seemed to notice. A third bell rang, signaling the group to raise their arms upward toward the figure on top of the obelisk, as if reaching in vain to grasp the hand reaching down to them from above. A final bell rang and the congregation, in well-rehearsed harmony, began to recite, what Bean could only describe as, a prayer:

"All Glory to One. We thank him for our lives, our shelter and our sustenance. His ways are just. His paths are straight. His truth is infinite. We pledge to him our lives, our fortunes, and our devotion. As he is One, so let us be one with Him."

The group repeated the mantra ten times. By the third or fourth count, Bean was able to get most of the words right, though he became more and more uncomfortable with the utterances each time he repeated them. A few moments after the final recitation was complete, yet another bell rang and the group began to disburse as quickly as it had formed. Bean was again swept up in the crowd that crept back toward the main gate endeavoring to exit the plaza. Just as he was about to pass through the gate himself, he felt a large hand firmly grip his left shoulder.

He turned around, staring up into the face of a man who said, in a low, stern voice, "You are not who you appear to be. You must come with me now."

Without another word, the man moved his hand to the back of Bean's neck, forcefully directing him through the gate. When he wanted Bean to go a certain direction, he applied the appropriate pressure to his neck, like the joystick on one of Bean's video games. Bean listened for instructions from Maximus, but heard nothing. He wondered if he had been crushed by the pressure of the man's hand on his collar. Without Maximus' guidance, he decided it best not to resist, realizing he could not likely outrun the man, nor did want to draw any more attention to himself than necessary. Besides, he rationalized, if he was indeed caught, they would likely take him to where Wart was being held. Once he was back with his younger brother again, he would then figure out how best to escape.

After a time, the man turned Bean from the main procession down a side street. In the middle of the third block, the pair stopped in front of one of the indistinguishable homes lining the road.

"This is it," snapped the man. "Get inside."

The number on the home read "**13-6**." The door swung open and Bean was pushed forcefully through the entrance.

"Sit," barked the man, pointing to a small table in the corner of the room, flanked by two wooden chairs.

"Listen, this is all a misunderstanding," started Bean.

The man put his finger up to his lips. Bean thought it best not to press the issue and obediently sat silently in one of the chairs.

Bean was now able to take in the full measure of the man for the first time. Standing over six feet tall, his blond hair was pulled back tightly, ending in a pony tail that went down about a foot on the man's back. He had a large pointed nose, his forehead severely sloped on the same angle as his pronounced beak. Lacking much of a chin, his face had the overall appearance of a traffic cone. It struck Bean for a moment that if he could unloose that ponytail, it might release the man's forehead and chin and give him a more natural appearance.

Bean was also able to make an examination of the inside of the home. It consisted of one room, each wall twenty feet apart. The floor was dirt, yet somehow felt cleaner than the kitchen floor at his own home. On the walls hung only one picture - the portrait of a man that appeared to be the same person from the statue in the City Square. One, thought Bean. There were two beds, each on opposite sides of the room, one slightly larger than the other. A large trunk lay at the foot of each of the beds and appeared to contain the possessions of the inhabitants, sparse as they appeared to be. Around the small bed was a tall, three-paneled divider consisting of a wooden frame draped with the same material of which their clothing was comprised. It seemed the divider was intended to provide a modicum of privacy for the resident of that side of the room. The room in general was more meager in decoration than his bedroom at home, a significant accomplishment. Looking up, he saw a hole in the roof two feet square that allowed for some sunlight to enter into the dwelling. A small oil lamp on the table likely provided light for the inhabitants during the evening hours.

Bean's attention was drawn back to the man as he pulled up a chair and sat directly in front of him, staring him straight in the eyes for what seemed an eternity. Bean became uncomfortable under the weight of the man's gaze and began to fidget in his seat.

"So, what are we going to do with you? What to do, what do?" the man repeated pensively as he stared up at the ceiling. "I suppose we could turn you in to the City Governors. Likely would be some pretty severe consequences for an impostor infiltrating the City."

The man looked at the floor and shook his head solemnly as if pondering the awful fate of such an impostor.

"I certainly can't let you go. Who knows what kind of trouble you would get into, and it would no doubt get traced back to me."

The man paused and again muttered, "What to do?"

Bean interrupted, "If I may sir, might I suggest..."

"I'd be quiet if I were you," said the man forcefully. "You're in no position to be making any suggestions."

The man again stared at him, occasionally mumbling, "What to do?" Finally, he stood up in front of Bean.

"Well, I hate to do this, but I'm afraid it's the only thing that can be done."

He reached out suddenly, grabbing Bean by the chest and raising him onto his feet. Releasing his grip, the man lifted his arms in the air. Bean turned and braced himself, expecting to be struck. Instead, he found himself engulfed in a wild embrace. The man's arms, now wrapped firmly around his waist, swept him off the ground into the air, twirling him around like a rag doll and gently depositing him again on the ground. He grabbed Bean's face between his large hands, bending over to kiss him on both cheeks and then his forehead.

With a colossal smile on his face, the man, with Bean's cheeks still firmly squeezed between the vice grip of his hands, said, "Well if it isn't Benjamin James, live and in person. Welcome home my young friend, welcome home."

⁂

Maximus emerged from his hiding place, chirping with laughter.

"I'm sorry my boy, I couldn't resist. I see you've met Joshua," Maximus said as he hopped to the man's shoulder.

Bean, still reeling from the turn of events, finally began to process the joke.

"Ha, ha. Very funny Maximus," he said, both perturbed and relieved.

"It's so good to see you again," the man said eagerly as he took Bean's hand in his own and began shaking vigorously.

"Have we met?" questioned Bean with hesitation, trying unsuccessfully to release his hand from the man's grasp.

"Well yes, many years ago, not that you would remember, you were just a baby at the time," replied Joshua, finally liberating Bean's hand.

"You knew me as a baby? Do you know my parents?"

Joshua hesitated a moment, and Bean detected a hint of sadness flash across his face.

In an instant, the sorrow vanished and Joshua replied enthusiastically, "Why yes, of course. I know your parents quite well. We couldn't be any closer if we were actual family. Your father and I grew up together, and your mother... well, your mother is a very special woman."

"Can I see them?" Bean pleaded.

Joshua paused for a moment, choosing his words carefully.

"Unfortunately, that isn't possible right now." Seeing Bean's disappointment, he quickly continued, "Nevertheless, I promise I will do all I can to get you to them as soon as possible. But first, I understand you have a little brother that is in a bit of a predicament. I'm afraid there is not much time. I've learned he is being moved to One City mid-day tomorrow. If we are going to free him, we need to do it soon."

Just as Joshua finished speaking, the door swung open wildly, banging against the wall. The noise made Bean jump out of his chair. At first he could not make out the backlit face of the figure standing in the doorway. The form stepped into the room, the light from the opening in the roof illuminating the face of a young girl - the girl Bean had met in the forest. It was Seven Hunter!

Before anyone could speak, Seven turned to Joshua and declared angrily, "What is he doing here? Are you trying to get us all killed?"

Joshua rose quickly and tenderly placed his hands on Seven's shoulders.

"I'm sorry, but it is our sacred duty. There is no other way."

"There's always another way," Seven retorted sharply as she broke free from Joshua's hands. You'd know that if you cared as much about your family as you do about the stupid prophecy."

"I'm sorry you feel that way," said Joshua sympathetically as he walked toward Seven and cupped her face in his hands. "I've told you that you don't need to be a part of this. I would never do anything to hurt you, but it is the only way."

"Well it's too late for that now, isn't it? If you get caught, I don't suppose that One will be too lenient on your family, even if I am just your niece. You have made my choice for me, just like father did," Seven said with fire as she again broke free from Joshua's touch.

She walked across the room and sat violently on one of the chests, staring down at the floor. Joshua gazed on Seven with heartbreak in his eyes. Bean had seen that same look in his father's eyes many times in the years since Katherine's disappearance.

After a few moments, Bean said cautiously, "Look, I don't want to put anyone in danger. This isn't your fight," and got up to leave.

His words seemed to snap Joshua out of his melancholy, and he turned quickly towards Bean with a wide grin on his face.

"That's where you are wrong my friend. It is very much my fight. It is all of ours. Your being here is the answer to many prayers. We had all but given up hope, and now here you are, standing in front of me. Blessed be the Ancient of Days. Surely, our delivery is nigh at hand."

Joshua again took Bean into his arms and gave him a giant hug.

"Listen," said Bean almost embarrassed, freeing himself from the embrace. "I'm not who you think I am. I'm just a kid. I'd like to help you, I really would, but all I'm concerned about is saving my brother and going home."

"And go home you will, my friend," replied Joshua, almost giddy. "We are all going home!"

Again a bell pealed across the City.

"We must leave for a while," said Joshua as both he and Seven instinctively began to walk toward the door.

"Wait," panicked Bean, "you can't just leave us here!"

"You'll be alright with Maximus," reassured Joshua. "I recommend you get some rest. We have a busy night ahead of us."

With that Joshua and Seven left the home and closed the door behind them.

Chapter 13
The Plan

The freshly risen sun shone directly into Bean's eyes, forcing him to squint in order to see the path in front of him. He once again found himself walking towards the center of Seven City, this time his wrists firmly bound behind his back. Joshua walked beside him, his right hand positioned on the back of Bean's neck, directing him towards the City Plaza in the same manner he had directed Bean to his home less than twelve hours before.

Bean hadn't had much sleep, being forced to share one of the small beds with Joshua, whose long skinny limbs jabbed Bean whenever it seemed he was about to doze off. Not that he could have slept much anyway. His mind rehearsed time and again the plan to free Wart that the group had devised upon Joshua and Seven's return.

The two entered the gate to the Square. Bean could see no one, but sensed he and Joshua were not alone. Most of the buildings in the Square were elaborately and ornately decorated, except for one located in the farthest corner. It was a substantial, square, windowless structure, made of what appeared to be black stone. It had a single, large metal door facing the Plaza with a small square opening interlaced with three vertical bars. He knew from Joshua's description the night before that this was the prison for Seven City. Looking at the building, his heart jumped at the thought of young Wart - all alone - in the dark, foreboding structure. Any fears Bean had prior to entering the Square washed away with this grim realization. He must free Wart, no matter the cost.

As Bean and Joshua approached the prison door, two large men armed with crossbow-like weapons emerged from the shadows on each side of the prison. Bean hesitated impulsively, looking backward for an escape, only to see two more large men a few feet behind, their crossbows aimed directly at his chest. Joshua's grip tightened on Bean's neck, and the pair resumed their approach to the prison.

"Found this one poaching fish at Nine Pond," Joshua said matter-of-factly. "Couldn't tell me where he lived and didn't have any identification. Figured he'd be good for a few promotions."

"We'll see," replied one of the guards. "Leave him. We'll take it from here. One thanks you for your vigilance."

"Just doing my part," said Joshua as he again squeezed Bean's neck in an attempt to give one final bit of encouragement. He then turned Bean over to the guards and quickly began walking back toward the gate.

Bean was moved brusquely inside the prison. The interior of the building consisted of one large square room containing a sizeable cell in the center that was divided into four equal, smaller cells. They were empty except for a small body lying asleep on a cot in the cell to Bean's right. He could tell by the shape of the blanket it was Wart.

One guard unlocked the cell nearest to the prison entrance and the other began to usher Bean through the opening, but was stopped in his tracks by a deep, gravelly voice booming from the corner of the room.

"Hold it right there!"

Bean turned towards the sound. The morning sunlight through the prison door had not yet reached the corners of the room and he peered into the darkness to identify the speaker. He could detect only the lumbering movement of a massive dark figure as it rose from a chair and slowly stepped into the light. Bean instinctively took a step backward as a massive grizzly bear appeared and began to approach him. In a panic, he looked up at one of the guards, pleading with his eyes to allow him to run. To his surprise, the guard seemed unphased by the sudden appearance of the bear. He simply tightened his grip on Bean's arm sufficiently to match his prisoner's effort to flee.

The bear waddled slowly on all fours towards Bean, emitting a small grunt with each step, as if incurring considerable effort to move its gigantic frame. The creature stopped in front of him, stretching its neck out so its head was only a few inches from Bean's face. Bean's body clenched as he closed his eyes and leaned back as far as he could in a vain attempt to avoid the bear's considerable teeth. The bear moved its nose up and down his body, sniffing vigorously.

After a time, the bear completed its inspection of Bean and rose up on its hind legs. As big as the beast seemed on all fours, it now seemed to Bean it had tripled in size as it stood in front of him.

"Leave us," roared the bear.

Immediately, the two guards turned and exited the building, leaving Bean alone with the massive animal.

The bear again lowered itself down on all fours with the force of a large oak being felled. It breathed heavily as the exertion of rising on two legs had taken a significant toll. At the end of each breath, the bear would involuntarily release a muffled growl.

After a few moments, it had sufficiently regained its lungs and snarled, "I know what you are up to. Did you think you could fool me?"

Bean panicked. Could the plan be foiled already? Did Wart tell the bear what he looked like?

Able to salvage some of his composure, he replied quizzically, "I... I don't know what you mean."

"Silence!" boomed the bear. "I will not be mocked!"

The bear paused again, Bean fidgeting under its icy glare. He could see oozing gobs of saliva beginning to form on the corners of the beast's mouth, and Bean began to wonder if he was about to be its next meal.

"Raise up your clothing," growled the bear.

"What do you mean?"

"Do it now!" roared the bear, the force of its breath almost knocking Bean backward.

Bean reluctantly reached down and slowly lifted up the pullover, revealing his bare legs.

"I knew it," the beast exclaimed as it raised its claws and expertly sliced off the package strapped to Bean's right leg.

It ripped open the bundle, revealing a large fish.

"Fishing without permission is punishable by death," snarled the bear.

"Please sir," pleaded Bean. "I was hungry. Nobody will miss one fish."

"Tell it to the Governors," the bear said sharply, raising its giant paw and swatting Bean on the shoulder, the force sending him sprawling head over heels into the jail cell.

The bars slammed shut behind him, and Bean slowly began to raise himself off the floor. Looking up, he found himself staring directly into the wide eyes of Wart who had awoken during the commotion. Bean ever so slightly shook his head and directed Wart with his eyes to remain silent. He worried the bear would detect the look of recognition from Wart, but the bear's attention was now fully focused on the fish as it returned to its seat in the corner of the building. Bean lay on his cot, listening to the sound of the bear sloppily devouring its newly acquired meal.

He stared up at the ceiling - waiting. It would be at least an hour before the poison killed the bear.

The bell rang at the regularly appointed hour for what Joshua called, "Morning Devotion." Before long, the Square was again filled with the inhabitants of Seven City as they gathered around the black obelisk and the statue of One. In the prison, Bean's heart quickened as he rose up on his elbows. There had been no sound from the corner of the room for some time now.

He whispered to Wart, "Get ready, it's time to go."

"Go where, Bean?" Wart queried annoyingly. "Maybe you didn't notice, we're in a jail with a humongous bear sitting in the corner."

"The bear is no longer a problem. Don't worry, I have a plan."

In the Square, the group was just finishing their final recitation when a loud shriek pierced the air. The crowd turned in unison toward the direction of the sound to find a small hooded figure standing on the east wall.

When all eyes were upon the shadowy form, it yelled in a high-pitched voice, "Death to One! Long live the Ancient of Days!"

With that, the mysterious being pulled a massive arrow from the sheath on its back, set it afire with a small torch at its feet, and pulled back the string on one of the large cross-bow weapons the prison guards had pointed at Bean hours before. The tiny figure was almost dwarfed by the weapon, but the shooter handled it deftly, taking steady aim and letting fly the flaming arrow toward the center of the group where it found its intended target - the midpoint of the large black obelisk. The arrow struck with such force it penetrated the surface several inches, sending out a spider web of tiny fissures radiating from the entry point. The arrow tip imbedding itself into the obelisk, a small fire began to grow and, within just a few moments, the entire monument burst into flames.

A wave of heat from the fire quickly swept over the crowd, followed shortly thereafter by a surge of panic as the large gathering began to sense the danger of the situation. At first the mass of people moved in a slow, orderly fashion toward the gate, but as fear gradually enveloped the group, the scene became one of havoc and confusion as the mob scrambled to vacate the Plaza.

In an instant, a cadre of guards appeared, their attention focused on the stranger on the wall. Almost before the first arrow struck the obelisk, a host of barbed missiles were tracking back towards the shooter. The hooded figure leapt from the wall just as a wave of projectiles penetrated the space that was, just a moment before, occupied by the mysterious archer.

Outside the wall, Maximus waited for the guards watching the prison to rush towards the pandemonium in the Square, momentarily leaving the building unguarded. Doing his best to avoid detection, he quickly flew from the back of the prison and darted through the small opening in the door. Landing softly on one of the bars in Bean's cell, he chirped cheerfully, "Good morning, my boys. I hope you've enjoyed your stay, but I believe we best be on our way."

"Maximus is your plan?" groaned Wart incredulously.

"By all means, you're quite welcome to maintain your current accommodations, my dear Warren," snapped Maximus.

"There's no time for your fighting," said Bean tersely. "Maximus, get the keys, the bear is in the corner," he directed while pointing toward the dead beast - at least he hoped it was dead.

Maximus rushed to the corner of the room, skillfully lifting the keys off the table and returning them to Bean who unlocked first his, and then Wart's, cell.

"Great, now what? There has to be ten guards surrounding this place," grumbled Wart.

"Let's hope not," said Bean as he opened up the door of the prison to a scene of pure chaos.

Joshua was right about the obelisk. It was made of a highly flammable, polished coal and the entire structure had erupted in a mass of flames when struck by Seven's arrow. The firestorm was now lapping at the statue atop the obelisk, giving

One a frighteningly hellish appearance. People were running in every direction. Smoke from the fire filled the air, adding to the mass of confusion. Bean looked to his left and right. The plan had worked, the guards had abandoned their posts in an attempt to try and control the frenzied mob.

"Follow me," he commanded his brother in a tone of confidence and authority that took Wart off guard and left him helpless to obey. He trailed Bean as they began to make their way through the crowd toward the gate. Several times it seemed the boys would be swallowed up and trampled in the throng, but eventually they were able to make their way to the entrance. Exiting the Plaza, Bean took a sharp right turn and headed down the street adjacent to the wall. Immediately Joshua and Seven joined them on either side.

The group quickly made their way back to Joshua's home, but, as they approached the door, Joshua told Bean and Wart to remain outside. Joshua and Seven entered the home for a brief moment, reappearing with what appeared to be four small knapsacks.

"Aren't we going in?" questioned Bean.

Joshua put his hands gently on Bean's shoulders and spoke softly.

"No Ben, it has begun. There is no going back for us now. They will quickly realize only a hunter could have performed such a shot as to hit the obelisk from the wall. It won't be long before they search the homes of all hunters. If we are discovered, there will be no more prison - we will be executed on the spot. We must leave Seven City now."

"Can't unlight the fire," said Seven disdainfully as she shoved one of the packs forcefully into Bean's chest, almost knocking him backwards.

The group quickly made their way towards the eastern border of the City and through the fields. Approaching the forest line, they were met by one of the guards that had been hastily dispatched in an effort to seal off potential escape routes.

The guard raised his hand and shouted, "Stop, no one is allowed to..."

The arrow penetrating his neck stopped him mid-sentence, and the guard slunk to the ground, lifeless. Seven approached the dead body, placed her foot on the side of the guard's head and reached down, yanking the small metal shaft back through his neck. She quickly knelt down beside the body and began wiping the blood off the arrow onto the grass. After a moment she looked up and noticed the open mouths and wide eyes of Bean and Wart staring down at her. Seven stood calmly, resleeved her arrow in the sheath behind her neck, and said matter-of-factly.

"You better get used to it."

With that, she turned and led the group into the darkness of the forest.

Chapter 14

Escape

A heavy silence shadowed the group as it moved through the forest. Wart clenched Bean's hand the moment Seven killed the guard and he had no intention of letting go anytime soon. Seven walked with her head down, her earlier bravado melting away into near tears. Only Joshua seemed to be unphased by the events of the past few hours, walking with what could only be described as a bounce in his step.

There was little time for rest. Joshua explained that hunting parties would be formed quickly, and once they found the dead guard, it would not be difficult for them to know which way the group had gone. Though Joshua and Seven were experts at hiding their own tracks, it was impossible for them to make the entire group invisible under such a rush. They now only had time on their side, which meant breaks were few and far between. Joshua said they had to make it to the eastern edge of the occupied zone. Bean was not in a mood to ask what or where that was.

Bean would occasionally glance at Wart. The recent perilous events had brought with them a realization that he really did love his little brother. He had just risked his life to save him, something he never imagined himself doing a few short days ago. He also felt a deep sense of pride in the success of the plan he had helped develop, keeping his cool in the most frightening of circumstances and performing like a superhero out of one of his comic books. He wanted nothing more than to return home, but couldn't help but love what he had become in this magical place.

After a time, Maximus returned from one of his reconnaissance flights and rested upon Bean's shoulder.

"Well done my good man. Great show back there indeed. And," turning to Wart, "as much as I'm loath to admit it, Warren my boy, you exhibited some exemplary bravery."

Wart simply shrugged his shoulders as he continued to walk, looking down at the ground before him.

"You were pretty exemplary yourself, Maximus," replied Bean. "It was nice to have someone who could fit through the bars. I'm pretty skinny but I don't think I could have squeezed through there. Your family will be very proud of you."

Maximus was awkwardly quiet, and Bean realized he may have said something wrong.

"Look, I'm sorry Maximus, I didn't mean to offend you."

Maximus replied softly, "No, my boy, don't be sorry. It's just that - I have no family. I am one of a kind you see. All of my kin were killed in the great battle. I was very young at the time. They would not let me fight."

"I'm so sorry Maximus. I had no idea."

"It's nothing my boy, don't give it thought, I certainly don't. I like to concentrate my attention on the future, and right now our future is very tenuous. I must again be on my way to see if we're being tracked."

Maximus flexed his legs to take flight from Bean's shoulder.

"Wait Maximus," Wart said as he lifted his eyes from the ground and looked at the small bird on Bean's shoulder.

"I... I'm sorry too."

Maximus was taken aback momentarily by the unexpected display of compassion from Wart. He hopped down to Wart's shoulder.

"Thank you my friend. I am sorry for how I've treated you. I can get a little full of myself at times to be sure. What say we start off on a new foot, or talon as the case may be? I believe we are destined to become very good friends you and I. Who knows, perhaps one day you and your brother will be my family."

With that Maximus darted into the air and flew back in the direction the group had come.

Not more than a minute had passed before Maximus reappeared, chirping frantically, "Make haste, make haste! They are upon us, make haste!"

Turning to see Maximus, Bean felt a rush of air past his right ear, followed immediately by an arrow striking the heart of a tree directly behind him. Seven grabbed him and Wart and pushed them violently onto the ground.

"Stay down," she shrieked.

Seven rolled across the pathway, taking cover behind a neighboring tree. In the blink of an eye she was launching arrows from the contraption on her forearm back towards, what as yet, was an unseen enemy. Amidst the panic and confusion, Bean couldn't help but marvel at the speed with which she retrieved the small dart-like arrows, placed them along her forearm in a wooden slot, pulled back a metallic spring near her elbow, and released the trigger by squeezing a vice-like grip that fit snuggly in her hand.

Joshua took cover behind a boulder and was also shooting arrows back through the forest from a similar, larger device attached to his left arm. After a moment, both Joshua and Seven ceased firing. Bean looked at Seven who was focused intently behind them, trying to make out her targets, her "arm bow" ready to fire at even the slightest movement. Her chest was heaving, but she didn't make a sound.

An eerie silence swept over the group; Bean's breathing and Wart's soft whimpering the only sounds. After a time, penetrating through the quiet, came the piercing chirp of a bird. Seven immediately adjusted her target toward the direction of the sound and let an arrow fly. Bean knew it had found its target when a cry of pain rose from amongst the trees. After a few moments, more chirping, and again Seven fired an arrow, as did Joshua. Another audible groan. It quickly dawned on Bean that Maximus was letting Joshua and Seven know precisely where their targets were. He could now hear the sound of several arrows being released, but nothing struck near the group. Bean guessed the hunting party had focused their attention on shooting the small creature that was divulging their position. Several more chirps were followed by an on-slaught of arrows from Seven and Joshua.

Then, another sound stabbed Bean's soul with the force and cruelty of an arrow. Not the chirping of a bird, but a faint, high piercing shriek.

Bean instinctively jumped to his feet yelling, "No Maximus! No!"

Seven whispered harshly, "Get down! You're going to get yourself killed!"

Another arrow hummed past, narrowly missing Bean and shattering as it struck the ground behind him. Bean fell to the earth, "Maximus," he muttered again and again as he buried his face into his hands. He knew what the sound meant - Maximus was dead.

"There's no time for that now, I'm almost out of barbs. There are at least ten more hunters back there. Get ready to run," said Seven urgently.

Joshua appeared behind the boys.

"On the count of three, you must get up and run like you've never run before. Seven and I will be right behind you."

Almost before Bean could process what was happening, Joshua yelled "Three!" He and Wart jumped to their feet, while Seven and Joshua simultaneously began sending a volley of arrows back at the hunters.

Bean and Wart crashed frantically through the bushes and branches that lined the path, Bean dragging Wart behind him. He had lost his little brother before and was not about to let it happen a second time. He could feel Seven and Joshua following and could hear the occasional arrow being shot back toward the hunters. Eventually the sounds ceased, and Bean assumed both Joshua and Seven were out of ammunition. The hunters had apparently come to the same realization and were now approaching the group with reckless abandon, letting out terrible sounding screams that seemed to get nearer with each passing second. Bean felt like he was being chased by a pack of wild animals, which, for all he knew, may actually be the case. The arrows from the hunters now came closer and closer to finding their targets, and Bean knew it would only be a matter of time before one found its mark.

Joshua swooped in from behind and grabbed the two boys by the collar, turning them from the path and plunging into the thick brush of the forest. They continued to run blindly through the foliage for a few hundred feet until they reached a large thicket. Joshua, in mid-run, lifted each boy by the back of his neck and leapt into the center of the brush with a crash. The twigs and leaves settling around them, the three lay on the ground, their faces pressed against the earth. Though unnecessary, Joshua raised a finger to his lips directing the boys to be silent.

They lay and listen, the long grass licking at Bean's face. The shrieks of the hunting party were now gone. Bean strained to see through the greenery surrounding him and, after a time, he spotted the figure of a man slowly approaching where the group was hiding. He could feel Joshua's muscles tense and could just make out the sound of him unsheathing the dagger strapped to his calf. It would only be a moment before Joshua sprang from the bush to fight the hunter - who was now just a few feet away - to the death. The hunter paused in front of the bush long enough to make a sharp whistling sound. It was clear he was signaling for the others. Bean knew they'd been found and the end was near.

At the very moment the hunter finished whistling a second time, an orange flash crossed through Bean's field of vision, and, in an instant, the hunter vanished. To Bean's immediate left rose a terrifying growl, followed by the frightened shrieks of what he knew was the hunter being attacked by some creature. He strained to witness the clash through the bushes. While he couldn't make out the entire animal, the orange and black stripes were unmistakable. Though most of his vision was obstructed, what he could see made his stomach lurch, as he watched the tiger's massive teeth rip into the hunter's neck. The screams stopped... for a moment.

Joshua leapt from his spot, yelling for the boys to stay put. For the next few minutes, the sounds of battle echoed across the forest. Finally, calls from the hunters for retreat rang out, then silence. Bean and Wart lay in the bush, not daring to move or speak. After a few moments, the two could hear someone approaching their hiding spot.

"It's okay boys, you're safe now, come on out," rang Joshua's familiar voice.

Bean and Wart slowly stood up, Wart's head just able to peak out over the top of the bushes.

Bean took in the scene in front of him. There was Joshua and Seven, surrounded by three tigers, two lions, five wolves and - a warthog?

Chapter 15
The Garden

The newly formed company hadn't walked for more than a half mile when the forest gave way to an open expanse of rolling meadow filled with marvelous vegetation and stunning waterscapes. As Bean emerged from the tree line, he instinctively raised his hand to shield his eyes from the brilliant colors flooding his senses. While the forest was magnificent, the scene that now unfolded before him quite literally took his breath away, and he had to stop for a moment to gather himself.

Where the forest had been a mélange of color and flora, each area of the meadow now unfolding before him had its own uniform plant life and pigment. The fields expanded like an ocean for as far as he could see, each area aflutter with activity. Everywhere Bean looked, he could detect movement of one kind of animal or another. The tiger, Ronar, who appeared to be the leader of the patrol that had fortuitously rescued Bean's little group, called the meadows, the "Garden." Bean could understand why, as every last inch seemed to be intricately cared for and manicured.

Dotting the landscape were crystal blue pools of water of various shapes and sizes. Small rivers and streams were interwoven between each pool like the shoelaces on one of Bean's sneakers. Atop virtually every hilltop was a fountain of water springing from the earth itself, which cascaded down the hillside in waterfalls of various form and contour, finally coming to rest in one of the pools. The entire area was bathed in the soft sounds of babbling water.

Immediately to Bean's left was a batch of small trees, each with long, wide palm fronds that were themselves interspersed with bright pink flowers tumbling in a string that almost reached the ground. To his right were thirty or forty small bushes with broad green leaves, each with a long yellow tongue-like flower sticking from its base, giving the plant the overall appearance that it was somehow making fun of him. Farther ahead, he noticed a fifty foot square area comprised of tall thin trees with dark purple spikes shooting from the top, so as to resemble a chubby violet porcupine perched atop a long pole. Flowers and grasses filled every available space that wasn't otherwise occupied by a tree, bush or plant. Bean particularly liked the bright red artichoke like bulbs from which a long black spire emerged and atop of which a lavender flower burst forth like a 4th of July firework. Large trees speckled the landscape as well, though not nearly as numerous as in the forest. Most had massive trunks that were completely covered in long, thin, green leaves mimicking animal fur. Atop the trees were ten to fifteen enormous branches spiraling outward from the center, creating an umbrella of shade fifty feet in diameter.

The group, which now included Bean, Wart, Seven, Joshua and their new animal companions, continued to make their way through the meadow to no particular destination that Bean could determine. Their pace was slowed as one of the tigers and a wolf had suffered large lacerations from their altercation with the hunters, but the urgency to move forward that existed in the forest was now absent and the group seemed content to make their way at a more leisurely pace that accommodated the injured. Both Bean and Wart welcomed the slower march as well. After the exhausting events of the day, Bean had resigned himself to whatever Joshua or the animals had in store for him. He only hoped sleep would be a part of his near future.

Every so often the group would encounter small dwellings, but they were crudely constructed and seemed to be more for shelter from the sun than for actual living accommodations. Bean would occasionally see another human, but they were few and far between. Passing the various animal inhabitants along the way, some that Bean recognized from his world and some he had never before seen, they would casually look up, give a nod, and proceed with their activities. It struck him as odd that some of the smaller animals did not appear to be the least bit concerned that so many beasts of prey were within just a few feet of them as they passed by. It then occurred to him for the first time that he himself was walking next to eleven animals that could rip him to shreds in short order. A frightening scenario for any human, let alone a young boy, but Bean felt strangely at ease.

Every hundred yards or so would be a new type of flower or bush, each one more brilliant and beautiful than the next, bearing the most unique and spectacular fruits or berries. Blooms leapt in every direction and in every conceivable shade, each fighting to outshine its brothers. The colors were so vivid it seemed to Bean he could actually taste them simply by looking at them. Apparently, Wart was having similar thoughts. Passing a small tree from whose branches were hung strings of bright orange fruit ending in pointed, green spikes interlaced together like a zipper, he could fight off his hunger no longer and grabbed one of the succulent pieces. Bean tried to stop him, but Ronar raised his paw and said it was all right for Wart to eat it and apologized for not offering something sooner. He motioned for Bean to have some as well. It wasn't until now that he realized he had not eaten all day, and he quickly grabbed a piece and devoured it. The flavors exploded in his mouth with an intensity that was at first disconcerting and then insatiable. The juices dripped down his chin as he couldn't help but to shove almost the entire piece of fruit into his mouth, followed quickly by another.

Joshua asked Ronar, "Does the meek and lowly one yet live?"

"He is becoming more feeble, but he is very much alive," responded the massive Tiger.

"We need to see him as soon as possible," Joshua replied, with an air of excitement that was excessive, even for him.

"I'm afraid that is impossible. You have been away for many years, Joshua. We were friends before, and may yet be friends once more, but I cannot grant you access to the meek and lowly one until you are able to demonstrate your loyalty to us once again."

"Your faithfulness is your strength my friend. I hope to prove my loyalty to you shortly, but for now, it is imperative we see the meek and lowly one. It simply cannot wait."

Joshua caught himself a bit and looked around out of habit to see if any unfriendly ears were listening. He continued on in a hushed tone, "Ronar," gesturing towards Bean, "our deliverance is at hand."

A look of incredulity crept across Ronar's broad face. The other animals that had up to this time been paying little attention to the conversation between Ronar and Joshua, suddenly raised their heads and looked at Bean. He was not sure what Joshua meant by what he had said, but it was clear to him the animals most certainly did.

Ronar paused and seemed uncertain as to how to process this new information.

"There is not much time," Joshua said. "Those hunters were only the beginning. Once One is apprised of the events in Seven City, it won't take him long to realize what is happening. We must take the boy to see the meek and lowly one, and we must do it now!"

Ronar's apprehension quickly dissipated and the massive beast slowly closed his eyes, bowing his head for a moment as if in great reflection. Suddenly, all was quiet as the entire Garden seemed to mystically recognize Ronar's unspoken need for silence. Just as Bean began to feel a bit uncomfortable, the big cat finally raised its head.

"Joshua, I feel the truth of your words."

He stepped toward Bean. Ronar was so large he could almost look him level in the eye, even while on all fours.

"Son of man, my friend Maximus sacrificed his life for yours. If he believed in you - and Joshua believes in you - that is sufficient for me. I will take you to see the meek and lowly one."

Ronar suggested the group get some much needed rest before proceeding on to the meek and lowly one. Just the mention of sleep triggered a wave of fatigue that swept mercilessly over Bean. He had been up since before dawn, with only a few hours of sleep the night before. It seemed it was weeks ago that he had freed Wart from the prison when, in actuality, it had been that very morning. He looked around and timidly asked Ronar, "is the place we will be sleeping very far?"

"Not far at all Benjamin. You are standing on it," replied Ronar. Bean looked down quizzically.

"I'm afraid my friend is used to somewhat different accommodations," said Joshua whimsically. "Don't worry Benjamin, you will never find a softer mattress than the grass under your feet here in the Garden. I, for one, haven't had a good night sleep since I left here."

After stuffing themselves on a buffet of delicious fruit, it wasn't long before the boys fell asleep. The warthog, who went by the name of Baffus, offered to let Wart use its ample belly for a pillow. Bean drifted off to sleep with a half-smile on his face, amused at the picture of Wart nestled up snuggly against the warthog.

Bean woke abruptly. Sitting up in an effort to reorient himself, he surveyed his surroundings and noted all of the party was sleeping nearby - except Seven. Scanning the horizon, he could make out her silhouette in the moonlight, sitting on the tip of a small rise a short distance away. He quietly stood and made his way toward the solitary figure. Approaching, he whispered Seven's name. Her back was to him and, upon realizing someone was nearing, she quickly raised her hands to wipe at her face. Bean slowly sat down beside her, careful not to sit too close as their interactions up to this point had not been what he could characterize as friendly.

"Are you okay?" Bean asked meekly.

Seven glanced quickly at Bean. He could see moonlight glistening off the wetness on her face where she had just wiped her tears.

"Of course I'm okay," she said defiantly, suddenly realizing her vulnerability. "I just couldn't sleep, that's all. There's a lot to think about. You think that by escaping the hunters you are safe? I hate to break it to you, but our troubles have just begun. It won't be long before One assembles all of his forces from the Seven Cities to come after you. And trust me, he won't stop until he gets you."

"But why? How does he even know about me? I left here when I was a baby. I'm just a nobody. How could I be a threat to him?"

"Believe me, no one thinks you are less of a threat to One than me," she said, shaking her head slightly. "Listen, I don't believe in it, but there was a supposed prophecy given that a pure child of Adam would be born and would deliver the inhabitants of Edinnu from One. It says that no blade shall harm the child and that the child's truth will destroy One. So, you can understand why One might not be your biggest fan."

"Well that's just crazy," mumbled Bean in amazement. "I'm nobody special. Besides, I've cut myself with knives plenty of times. We've got to tell everyone I'm not the kid they think I am."

"Don't you see, it's too late for that now. One thinks you are the Deliverer - not to mention Joshua. There will be no dissuading either. Whether or not you're the Deliverer doesn't even matter at this point. One won't stop until you're destroyed and Joshua and the others will do anything to make sure that doesn't happen, even if it means sacrificing their lives for yours."

The two sat in silence. After a while, Bean inched closer to Seven, reached out and touched her knee and said earnestly, "I'm sorry about this. I didn't mean to cause any trouble. I just want to go home to my mom and dad."

He just managed to get the last words out before he began to cry.

Seven sat there awkwardly, not knowing how to comfort him. Finally, she reached around and grabbed his shoulder and pulled him close to her.

"Listen, I'm sorry for being so hard on you. I suppose I'm just angry... and maybe a little bit frightened. I was a small child the last time we went to war with One. My father was killed. After the truce, Joshua, my uncle, was called by the meek and lowly one to take me and live in Seven City where he could keep an eye on One's activities there. I just don't want to go through all of that again for nothing. It's not you that makes me angry, it's what you represent."

"Can't you just take me to the wall? I still have the key stone. Wart and I can go back home and this will all be over," Bean said pleadingly.

"You just don't get it do you. This will never be over until either you or One are dead. You might be able to escape to your world for a while, but he will find a way to get to you. Your mother did everything she could to keep you safe and far away from this place and yet, here you are. Whether you or I like it or not, there is no turning back."

The two sat again in silence for several minutes.

Finally Bean spoke earnestly, "Seven, if anything happens to me, will you watch out for Warren? He didn't deserve any of this. My parents couldn't bear losing another child."

Seven stiffened, "What do you mean another child?"

"Well, I had a sister. She disappeared. It almost killed my parents to lose her?"

"A sister?" Seven asked with a curiousness Bean had not seen before. "How long ago was this?"

"About six years, why?"

Seven sat very still, as if holding her breath. Eventually, Bean could feel her body relax again.

"Never mind. It's nothing."

As he began to press Seven, she abruptly stood and reached down to help him up.

"We've got a long journey tomorrow. We'd better get some sleep."

Finally, facing Bean, Seven could clearly see the fear and sadness in his eyes. For the first time since they met, she felt compassion for him instead of contempt, a wave of guilt sweeping over her as she realized what he must be going through. Even though he was three years her younger, Bean was already a few inches taller. She lifted his chin and cupped his face in her hands as she looked into his eyes intently.

"Don't be frightened Benjamin. In case you didn't notice, I'm the best shot in Edinnu. I won't let anything happen to you or Warren. I don't believe in the prophecy - but I believe in you. You have been very brave. We'll get through this together."

Bean was taken aback by this sudden kindness from Seven. It triggered a flood of emotion that had been dammed up by the events of the past few days. He melted into Seven's arms, sobbing. The two stood in the moonlit meadow in a warm embrace. For the first time in many years, each felt comforted.

Chapter 16
The Meek and Lowly One

Even with the magnitude of his present circumstances weighing heavily upon him, it was hard for Bean not to feel a certain sense of happiness and contentment as he walked along. The Garden had a wonderfully magical quality. Everything was so vibrant and full of life. Even Wart seemed to gain new energy as he frolicked blissfully to and fro with his new best friend Baffus. The porcine pair would stop every few hundred yards to eat something new and delicious, and the sounds of Wart's laughter and Baffus' grunts floated gleefully over the rolling hills of the Garden.

Bean noticed Seven was now never far from his side. The two rarely spoke, but he felt reassurance in her presence.

It soon became clear that word had spread among the general population of the Garden that the "Deliverer" had arrived, and animals and humans alike came to see Bean for themselves. He felt a distinct unease with so many animals gawking at him as he passed them by. After several years of making an annual trip to the Kansas City zoo with his family, he thought it ironic that he was now the attraction, and the animals were coming to see him. But everyone was very friendly and, after they had gotten a good look, returned to their various activities.

Venturing farther and farther into the Garden, the group encountered more dwellings. Most were small, simple structures and blended in so well with the surroundings that one could easily miss them if not paying close attention. From what Bean could tell, only the humans inhabited the homes, and it seemed the farther they walked, the human population increased dramatically. Even still, there was not one direction he could look where dozens of different types of animals did not appear before him.

As the vivid blue sky deepened into a rich purple dusk, Ronar announced to the group they had arrived, and only he and Bean could proceed on to see the meek and lowly one.

Joshua pulled Bean aside and said reassuringly, "Don't worry Benjamin, the meek and lowly one is very kind and wise. He can give you the answers you seek and will direct you to the right path."

Ronar and Bean walked the few hundred yards down a trail that led to a small, modest dwelling, similar to those he had passed along the way, differentiated only by the presence of two massive, jet black lions lying on either side of the entrance. Bean had not been frightened by any of the animals in the Garden, but these lions caused him to hesitate for a moment. One was missing an ear, and both had marks and scars indicating they had been through many battles. To Bean's relief, they appeared to be sleeping.

To the right of the dwelling was the largest tree Bean had yet encountered in Edinnu. The trunk was at least

15 feet in diameter, with three substantial legs protruding from the bottom like a tripod, so as to give the massive tree additional support. Unlike the other trees that were covered in vegetation, the bark was barren and grey with a smooth, glossy texture. The branches extended upward into the clear air like a towering skyscraper that could be seen from miles away.

As Ronar and Bean approached, the big cats drowsily lifted their heads. Ronar nodded at them both, and they again lowered their heads and closed their eyes. Ronar looked at Bean and motioned with his head toward the entrance.

"You may proceed."

Bean was unsure, but the tone of Ronar's voice seemed to him more of a command than a suggestion. Slowly pulling back the cloth that hung as a door, he carefully peered inside. The room was dark except for a small opening in the ceiling that let in a fading beam of sunshine, providing just enough light to see. Dug into the hillside, the back wall and a portion of each side of the home were comprised of earth. The room was small and appeared to be empty but for a small table and two chairs in the center. Bean walked into the middle of the room, nervously glancing around. At first appearance, he thought he was alone, and he prepared to sit in one of the chairs and wait for the meek and lowly one to join him.

A rustling in the corner of the room caught his attention.

"Welcome my son. This day has been long in coming."

Bean peered into the darkness trying to make out who - or what was speaking to him. The only features he could identify were, what appeared to be - two large rabbit ears? He thought the figure far too large to be a rabbit, although, at this point, he wouldn't be surprised at all if a 5-foot bunny did indeed appear before him. As the creature arose and crossed through the light from the ceiling, a donkey came into view.

Bean, surprised at seeing a donkey in front of him, stammered out, "I... I'm sorry to disturb you, I was told to wait here for the meek and lowly one."

"Well there is no need to wait any further. I am he who is called the meek and lowly one."

"Oh, I thought... I mean, I..."

"You were expecting a human, I'm guessing. It's quite all right my son. I know you come from the world where animals such as me are not able to speak. I'm sorry if this is disconcerting to you."

"No, I'm sorry. I just didn't..." Bean fumbled as he attempted to do a half bow, half curtsey. "I mean, forgive me your highness."

The meek and lowly one gave out a hearty, braying laugh.

"I think it a bit contradictory to call someone your highness whose name is the meek and lowly one. Please my child, be of comfort. I am no one to be nervous or afraid of. I am a friend. Please sit."

Bean tried to gather himself as he sat in one of the chairs.

"You are just as I imagined you would be," said the meek and lowly one with admiration as he lay himself on the ground at Bean's feet.

Regaining a degree of composure, Bean responded with a tone of frustration, "Everyone keeps telling me they know me and that I'm from here and... I don't even know where here is."

"I understand this is a very confusing and frightening time for you my child. The time has now come to resolve all of your questions. I will answer them to the very best of my ability. There is nothing I know that I will not tell you."

"Okay," said Bean resolutely. "Where am I?"

The meek and lowly one replied with a slight grin.

"Well, that is the easiest question of them all. You are in the garden that was planted eastward in Edinnu when the world began. Or as I believe you call it in your world - the Garden of Eden."

Chapter 17
Answers

"The Garden of Eden," Bean almost yelled back. "Theee Garden of Eden... like from the Bible?"

"The very same," the meek and lowly one responded with a hint of amusement.

"But that's just a story. You've got to be kidding me!"

"I assure you Benjamin, I am not joking," said the meek and lowly one, regaining a more serious tone. "You, my child, now find yourself at the center of all creation. The home of Father Adam and Mother Eve before they were cast out into the dark and desolate world. The place where man came to be, and where free will was born. The place of both the rise and fall of man. The place where lamb and lion lie down together."

Bean leaned back into his chair incredulous.

"The Garden of Eden," he murmured to himself, shaking his head in disbelief.

Contemplating the magnitude of what he was being told, he sat silently for a moment, then questioned, "But Adam and Eve were kicked out of the Garden. How come there are people and animals here?"

"Excellent question, Benjamin. Well, to be more precise, only Adam and Eve were expelled. The animals that were here committed no wrong and were never banished. They and their descendants have inhabited this place since the beginning. As for the humans, over the years, through various means and instruments, a few men and women have made their way back into the Garden. Those few have multiplied into what you see today. You must remember that when Adam and Eve were cast out, the Garden did not disappear, they were simply prohibited from returning. The Garden of Eden has always been here Benjamin, but in your world, because they cannot see it, they think it a myth or a fable."

Bean leaned forward with keen interest, rapt in the marvelous story unfolding before him.

"And how is it possible that I'm here?"

"The gateway to the Garden and your world has been, and always will be, the old rock wall near your home. When you were taken to your new family in the dark and desolate world, you were given a key stone to open the entrance into the Garden. When you rebuilt the wall and inserted the key, the gate unlatched, as it were, and here you are."

"Who took me to my world, was it my mother?" Bean asked eagerly.

The meek and lowly one looked down and sighed.

"Yes, your mother risked her very life to take you there. You were beloved by her. It took every last ounce of that love to give you away."

"But why... why did she have to give me up?"

The meek and lowly one paused again.

"About seven years ago there was a great and terrible battle between the forces of One and the true followers of the Ancient of Days. The battle was waged, in large part, because of the advent of your birth. I understand young Seven has informed you of the prophecy."

Bean wondered how the meek and lowly one could have known this, when suddenly, a burst of revelation.

"Wait, it can't be me. Woo hoo!" he shouted in joy as he leapt to his feet and did a small victory dance.

"You said the Great Battle was seven years ago. Well, I'm almost fourteen. Don't you see, you've got the wrong kid! There's no way that I'm the Deliverer - the math just doesn't work out. Now," Bean concluded with a triumphant air, "can my brother and I get outta here?"

The meek and lowly smiled with both a hint of mirth and sadness.

"I'm afraid it is not that simple my son. You see, time is a very peculiar thing. It is relative and specific to the sphere or plane of existence in which it is operating. From those few that have traversed back and forth between the Garden and the dark and desolate world, it has become evident that time is not measured equally in both places. I'm afraid I don't quite understand it myself, but it appears that roughly every year spent in the Garden is equal to two years in your world. So the math, in actuality, does indeed work."

Bean's prior exuberance melted into disappointment upon hearing the meek and lowly one's explanation and he sank back into his chair.

"Now, as I was saying," the meek and lowly one continued. "When it looked as if the forces of One were destined to prevail, Joshua helped your mother escape to the wall, and she crossed into your world. She had with her the only two key stones remaining. She left one with you and used the other to cross back into the Garden. When she returned to Edinnu, she crushed her key stone, hoping that by so doing, One would not be able to get to you and you would be safe."

Bean could restrain himself no longer, "My father and mother, are they here? Can I see them?"

The meek and lowly one slowly lifted his head and laid it tenderly on Bean's knee.

"My son, your father has passed through the veil. His body was killed in the Great Battle and is buried not far from this place. The veil is very thin here my child. I assure you, your father yet lives and is here with us now."

The meek and lowly one hesitated for a moment in reflection and began again.

"As for your mother, a more beautiful and kind woman never walked the Garden since Mother Eve. On her way back from taking you to the dark and desolate world, she was captured by One. She yet lives, but is imprisoned in One City. Many have died trying to rescue her. Her cause is lost... for now."

Bean fought against swelling tears. He did not know his father and mother, but the news of their fate struck him to the very core.

"After your escape, the True Believers, as we call ourselves, were able to withstand the attacks of One for a time and, with the main object of his desire now outside of his grasp, One eventually retreated with his forces to the Seven Cities, and there has been relative peace ever since. From that time, One has made every effort to find and destroy you, but you have been kept safe until now. Unfortunately, you did the majority of the work for him. By building the wall and using the key stone, you once again opened up the gate. To be sure, you are lucky to have survived. Once we were apprised of your efforts, we did everything we could to put a stop to your work. The nearer the wall came to completion, the thinner the gateway between the two worlds became. Some smaller animals were able to make it far enough into your world to send you messages and try and take down the wall. Apparently you were very stubborn. But no matter, I suppose it was always your fate to return here notwithstanding what anyone did, even your mother."

"A woman came to me in my room and warned me to leave. She was made up of hundreds of fireflies. Was that my mother?" Bean queried.

"I suppose that could be so. Even though she is in prison, it may have been possible for her to give a message to the fireflies. With the gateway opened, they could have made their way to you. As you can see, your mother never stopped caring for you."

"She was so beautiful," Bean mused to himself.

"Well, in that case, it was most certainly your mother. Her name is Dawn. All creatures in Edinnu are captivated by her. I think even One could not bring himself to destroy your mother, which is why he has kept her captive these years. Of course, his plan may simply be to use her to get to you in the event you ever returned to Edinnu."

"Who is One?" asked Bean quickly, not wanting to dwell on his mother's present circumstances.

"One is a pure son of Cain, the firstborn of Father Adam. Cain has walked the world since the time of his curse. Some of his descendants found their way back into the Garden. They felt then, and continue to feel now, that they were robbed by Father Adam of their rightful inheritance and began to wage war against the True Believers. That battle has waged for hundreds and hundreds of years. One is the most recent and vile of all Cain's descendants and has brought the Seven Cities under his thumb. He follows the plan of the Son of the Morning and has used secret signs and covenants prepared from the foundation of the world to destroy all opposition and consolidate his power. Sadly, we have become relatively help-less against him and he no longer considers us a serious threat, that is, with the exception of a child that it has been foretold will destroy him. And you are well aware of who that is."

"But what makes me so special?" Bean asked helplessly.

"The prophecy instructs that you are a direct descendant of the patriarchal lineage of Father Adam and the matriarchal lineage of Mother Eve. In other words, your father came only from the male birthright descendants of Father Adam and your mother only the first-born female descendants of Mother Eve. As such, you are the pure heir of Father Adam and Mother Eve. They were to live forever in the Garden... but then came the fall. As you quite literally have their blood coursing through you, for so long as you are here in the Garden, you too are immortal as they would have been had they remained. It is foretold only such a child will have the power to destroy One."

Bean blurted out, "Where did this stupid prophecy come from anyway? It sounds crazy to me."

"Yes, I suppose it does. But prophets can only say what Father tells them - that is, I can only say what Father tells me."

Bean looked at the meek and lowly one in disbelief, "You... you're the prophet? No offense, but - you're a donkey."

Showing no indignation or offense at the remark, the meek and lowly responded kindly, "I suppose it is strange to you. I am aware of how those of my family are treated and viewed in your world. But from the beginning, my kind has held a prominent place in the great and eternal plan of the Father. We were chosen to carry the mother of the Son before he was born and also to carry the Son into Jerusalem to perform the great and last sacrifice. Because of this role, that most evil serpent condemned us to be reviled and abased and to bear the burdens of man until the return of the Son."

Bean muttered, "I'm sorry, I didn't mean anything by it. This is all just so hard to believe."

"Belief is a hard thing for anyone my child. It is the greatest battle any of us will face. Just know this, your mother and father in your world believe in you as do your mother and father here. Your little brother Warren believes in you, Joshua and Seven believe in you, and I, a prophet, believe in you. But most importantly, deep within you, is a belief in yourself... that you are a child of the Father and through Him all things are possible. You grasp and cling at the idea that you are of no worth, while those who know and love you best are moving mountains to convince you otherwise. You value the harsh words of strangers above the very voice of God. Benjamin, the time has come for you to believe in your worth and your greatness. You must find that belief within you - or all is lost."

Bean sat for a moment, trying to let the past few minutes sink in, his hand impulsively stroking the forehead of the meek and lowly one. There would be no further point in arguing. As far-fetched as it all seemed, he knew there was no way out for him now. He was the Deliverer, and there would be no convincing those around him otherwise.

Finally, in surrender, he muttered, "Okay, I'll try my best. What now?"

"Now," the meek and lowly one said, "we prepare for war."

Chapter 18
War

The days and nights blurred together in a medley of commotion and preparation. Bean spent much of his time with Seven, who had taken it upon herself to teach him the basics of shooting an "arm-bow" and other basic hunting skills. He was quite pleased with his progress, though any words of praise from Seven were few and far between.

Bean noticed after his first few days in the Garden, there began to be a great influx of both humans and animals into the general area surrounding the great tree. The meek and lowly one explained that the outlying inhabitants were relocating to a more centralized position in an effort to protect themselves from the forces of One and to join all of the True Believers into one body. There had not, as yet, been any sign of One's troops gathering, but Bean was informed it was only a matter of time. The immigrants brought with them stores of food and whatever possessions they had, though it appeared most had very few belongings to begin with.

Bean spent many hours with the meek and lowly one. Particularly interested in learning about the key stones, he was informed the stones had been, "prepared from the foundation of the world for the Father's purposes." At one time there were known to be eight to ten stones and these were the general means by which humans had been able to return back to the Garden of Eden over the centuries. The meek and lowly one was only aware of one remaining key stone in either world - the one now in Bean's possession.

"If anything ever happens to that stone, it is unlikely you could ever again return to your home," the meek and lowly one said.

Bean was also informed him there were other stones in addition to the key stones, called "seer stones," through which the meek and lowly one received prophecy, including the one about Bean. After several days of pleading, the meek and lowly one finally agreed to let Bean view the seer stones. One of the stones was about the size of a small hen's egg. It was composed of layers of different colors passing diagonally through it. It was very hard and smooth as if it had been handled often over thousands of years. The other stone was also in the shape of an egg though not as large. It was made of a gray material, something like granite, but with white stripes running around it with a milky translucent glow. Bean asked to know how the seer stones worked, but the meek and lowly one quickly put them away and told him that if it be the Father's will, he would be shown how they functioned at a later time.

Wart spent much of his time with his new friend Baffus. Often, Bean would see them wrestling or playing some game on the rolling meadows. He was pleased Wart had a distraction from being away from home, but every time he would look at his brother, he felt a pang of guilt reminding him he was responsible for bringing him to this place. If anything happened to Wart, he could never forgive himself. Such a realization would jolt Bean back into the gravity of his present circumstances. But for that constant reminder, Bean would be in a wonderland, spending time with Seven and feeling more at home than he had ever felt in his life.

Joshua's days were largely spent in meetings with the meek and lowly one, Ronar and several others. He told Bean the group was the Council of War, and they were busy making preparations for the upcoming battle. At one point, Bean was invited to attend the meetings, but declined. He told Joshua it was because he had no experience in matters of war and would only be a nuisance. But, if he were to be truthful, he was simply doing his best to avoid coming face to face with the reality of what he knew was fast approaching. He much preferred his time spent with Seven and other less weighty activities.

With the end of Bean's second week in the Garden nearing, the first signs of the gathering of One's forces were sighted near the forest line. Even though he was many miles away, at night Bean could see hundreds of fires forming a dotted line of tiny lights along the edge of the forest.

"Is that them?" Bean asked Seven as she approached him from behind, placing her hand on his shoulder.

"Yes, and just the beginning I'm afraid. You've been to Seven City. There's about 10,000 or so that live there. It's by far the smallest of the Seven Cities. No doubt One will make everyone fight who is old enough to stand and hold a weapon."

Immediately upon the appearance of the fires, the activity around Bean's location increased dramatically. What few weapons the True Believers possessed, mostly rudimentary bows and arrows, were owned by the humans as most of the animals were simply incapable of using them. But the animals weren't without protection. Most had their own built in defenses, whether they be sharp teeth or claws or whatever else nature had seen fit to provide them. Some managed to cover themselves with make-shift armor or protective gear, though such protections were meager at best.

What the animals lacked in weaponry, they made up for in sheer diversity. Bean surmised it would be difficult indeed for any army to face an opponent comprised of so many shapes and sizes and with so many different skills and abilities. With that said, it was clear to him that due to the generally peaceful nature of the inhabitants he had encountered in the Garden, war was largely a foreign concept and he worried about what chance, if any, this rag tag group would have against what he surmised was a well-armed and well trained army.

Bean's carefree activities were severely curtailed upon the arrival of One's forces. It was generally acknowledged that, up to this time, Seven was informally acting as his bodyguard, but the two large black lions, Patel and Essig, that had previously been designated to protect the meek and lowly one, were now never far off. At night, Bean was required to sleep in a make-shift tent, which was guarded at all times by the lions. While it would have been difficult for any human to get to him at his current location, One did have many animals under his control, and Joshua was concerned One would use those animals to penetrate their defenses and kill Bean without having to be bothered with going to war.

With the number of campfires along the tree line growing, the mood at camp became increasingly somber as the specter of war rapidly approached. Tens of thousands of animals and humans had gathered together in a place where, just a few weeks before, there were only a handful of inhabitants. The area now had the feel of a bustling city from his world and was aflurry with activity. Other than Bean, everyone seemed to have a job to do, and they were busy doing it.

The faint sounds of trumpets slowly roused Bean from his slumber. Venturing out of his tent, he made his way to Joshua to see what the commotion was all about. When he arrived, Joshua was just leaving with Ronar and an elephant named Toth.

"And where are you off to today?" Bean said, using his best efforts to sound cheery.

"Well, well, if it isn't Benjamin James," retorted Joshua in a tone that exhibited a decidedly unforced happiness. "No doubt you are here to ask about all that racket from the forest this morning. Well, it's an invitation of sorts. One is requesting we send representatives to meet to discuss the terms of war, and that group is what you see before you now."

"That sounds dangerous."

"A bit I suppose," Joshua answered quickly, trying to dispel Bean's concerns. "But as evil and duplicative as One is, he is someone that takes war very seriously. I don't believe he would try anything - for now. However, after our meeting today, I would guess all bets are off."

"Then let me come with you," pleaded Bean.

"I'm afraid that would be unwise. Best that you be kept hidden at least for now. From a strategic standpoint, I'd prefer that your whereabouts remain a mystery. From a protection standpoint, I didn't say this meeting is without any danger at all."

Joshua could see the disappointment in Bean's eyes.

"I know you want to help and that you feel a great responsibility. Please trust in me for now. I will return before long and will give you a full report. Be patient. It won't be long before there is more excitement than all of us can handle."

Joshua returned as the setting sun slowly began to paint the horizon with various shades of purple, orange and red, promptly summoning Bean to meet with him and the meek and lowly one. There were several others at the meeting, some with whom Bean was well acquainted and others he had only met briefly during his time in the Garden. The meek and lowly one informed him the group comprised the Council of War, and they were called together to discuss Joshua's meeting with the representatives of One.

Joshua informed the group that the delegation sent from One consisted of two Caretakers and One's second in command who, not surprisingly, was called Two. The parties met in an open field, several hundred yards from the tree line, just far enough away from the forest to be out of the range of any weapons pointed their way. There was little discussion between the groups and their meeting lasted only a few minutes. Two simply handed a scroll to Joshua and indicated the document contained the terms upon which One would spare the lives of the "Outcasts" as he called them. Joshua replied in turn that it appeared his party had traveled a great distance for nothing, but he would deliver the letter to the meek and lowly one as directed. With that, the two camps parted ways and Joshua made his way back as fast as he could to report to the Council. Upon concluding his tale, Joshua produced the scroll from a pouch attached to his side.

The meek and lowly one bade him to read the letter to the group:

> To the one that calls himself "The Prophet," written by mine own hand.
> Sadly, your actions have once again brought our people to the brink of war. It has been 7 years since the Great Battle. Many of my people were killed in that fight, their blood forever upon your hands. Although it is clear that my forces outnumber yours and that the result of any further conflict would surely be decided in our favor, I have no wish to

sacrifice any more of the blood of my people in such an endeavor.

However, if you do not value your lives or the lives of your wives and children, and compel us to come against you, we will, once and for all, destroy you and cleanse this place from your unrighteous habitation. Divine justice will see to it that we are restored unto all the lands that you have obtained through deceit and treachery

You know within your hearts that our first parents robbed Father Cain of the birthright to which he was entitled. You know that he was falsely accused of murder and cast out from his rightful place to roam the dark and desolate world. You know that he was led back to this world by the divine hand of God and we, his descendants, are the rightful heirs to these lands. You know all these things, and yet you continue in your lies and defamations. We have tolerated your presence until now, because you are no threat to us, but the time of our benevolence is coming to an end.

I know that you are harboring an intruder into this land, a boy whom you call, "the Deliverer." By your own admission, he is an enemy to me and to the Grand Order. I do not fear him, for I fear no one. Yet, his presence has become a nuisance as many of the weak-minded in the Grand Order are easily led into incorrect paths. I will not al-low anyone or anything to bring instability to that which I and my fathers before me have worked so hard to build. The child is nothing to me, but his destruction has become requisite for the benefit of the whole.

Your choice is clear; give up the child, and you may continue your unrighteous occupation of this land in peace. If you remain stubborn in your adherence to a false god and incorrect traditions and refuse to deliver the boy, I will unleash an army of death and destruction upon your people as has never before been seen. We will rid this place of you once and for all. If you have any affection for your women and children, you will take action to prevent the awful atrocities that will surely fall upon them. I pledge to you that my forces shall not rest until every last creature among you is destroyed.

Perhaps you think your God can save you from the awful fate that awaits you. Yet I know that the true God does not favor your people over my people. We are a righteous nation devoted to the one and true path. I govern my people with equity and justice. Under my guidance, they are led in correct ways and are a diligent, industrious and obedient people. Surely God will aid us in your annihilation and grant unto us again what is rightfully ours.

Alas, I seek not your destruction, but my compassion and patience have come to an end. You, and you alone, are in control of the destiny of your people. I trust you care enough about them to save them from the most awful of fates.

You shall have until mid-day tomorrow to deliver the boy. If he is not brought to me by then, my armies will fall upon you until this land is made red with your blood.

I await the boy.

One

Joshua slowly rolled up the paper and placed it back in the pouch. All eyes in the room were focused intently on Bean, One's words hanging ominously in the air. Finally, from the corner of the room behind him, a lamb named Jalla softly spoke.

"Meek and lowly one... are you certain it is he?"

The meek and lowly one slowly rose off the floor, stood on all fours and walked reverently towards Bean. He came within a few inches of his face and looked Bean in the eye for what seemed several minutes, as if trying to gaze into the uttermost depths of his soul. Bean was relieved, as he was sure that, at last, the meek and lowly one would see he was not the "Deliverer," and that this nightmare could now be over.

Finally, the meek and lowly one quietly uttered, "I am certain."

Upon speaking the words, the meek and lowly one bowed his head and slowly bent his left leg until one knee was touching the ground, and he was kneeling in front of Bean. Almost simultaneously, the other members of the Council of War knelt in a similar fashion, forming a circle around him.

Bean stood there in silence.

Chapter 19
Shadows

Bean tossed and turned under the weight of his present circumstances. The magnitude of the situation rested fully upon him now, and he could no longer push what was about to transpire from the forefront of his mind. He had already seen some frightening and terrible things, but he knew it was nothing compared to what soon awaited him and his friends. He secretly hoped, when he awoke from his slumber, that he'd again find himself back at home in his bedroom and that his time in Edinnu would have been a dream. Finally, mercifully, he succumbed to sleep

Awaking in the middle of the night, he found himself still in his tent in the Garden. An eerie quiet hung in the air around him, producing a distinct heaviness upon his skin. He had grown accustomed to the sounds associated with the constant preparations for war, even during the night, but those sounds were noticeably absent now. Poking his head out the tent door, he was surprised to see his lion guards were no longer at their posts. Stepping outside, he widened his search over the horizon and quickly became aware that it was not just the lions - everyone had vanished.

His eyes were drawn to a small fire in a clearing a few hundred yards away, and he instinctively made his way toward the flame. Halfway to the fire, he became aware of a solitary figure sitting on a log next to the blaze. Sheer dread swept over his soul as he immediately recognized the personage as the horrible creature from his first night in the Garden - Mahan. He had spent every day since that encounter trying to convince himself the first meeting was merely a dream. Everything in him wanted to run, but as with his first confrontation, his legs were rendered useless, and he was compelled by an unseen force to move toward the creature until he could feel the warmth of the fire on his skin.

"Come and sit," came a voice that shook Bean to the core. He knew the voice emanated from the creature, though he did not move his mouth nor did he interrupt his steady gaze into the fire.

Bean was compelled to obey the voice and, in a moment, he found himself sitting next to the beast, his shoulder touching Mahan's right arm. Bean could feel the thick, matted hair and soot against his bare skin. The two sat staring into the fire, the hypnotic flames almost making Bean forget that he was sitting next to his worst nightmare.

After a time, Mahan slowly reached into a small pouch hanging from his neck and brought his hand forward into Bean's view. Unclenching his fist, Bean could see two small stones in the palm of Mahan's hand. Upon closer inspection, he noted they were the seer stones the meek and lowly one had previously shown him. Surprised that Mahan was now in possession of the stones, Bean struggled to ask how he got them, but was unable to open his mouth to speak.

Again the voice, "Look into the stones, they will show you what is to come."

Bean was already looking at the stones, but as he began to focus his eyes more intently, everything around him began to slowly disappear until he was enveloped by pure blackness. In a moment, the darkness began to fade, and he found himself again sitting by the fire. To his great relief, Mahan was now nowhere to be found.

The previous silence had been replaced by the sounds of far off groaning and weeping. At first, Bean thought he'd been transported back to the hell Mahan had shown him that first night, but in a moment he could see he was indeed still in the Garden. In addition to the fire directly in front of him, flames now dotted the entirety of the countryside. Confused and disoriented, he began to make his way back to his tent. He walked only a few yards before he nearly tripped on the mangled corpse of a small goat. Stumbling away in surprise at this gruesome discovery, he toppled headlong over the massive body of a tiger. Sprawled on his back, Bean turned to his right to see he was only inches from the head of the big cat. It was Ronar.

Bean scrambled to his feet in horror and ran to his tent, his path lined with dead and dying animals, as well as uniformed soldiers he could only assume were One's forces. The ground was literally littered with bodies, and he had to pick his way through the slaughter to avoiding stepping on them. Arriving at his tent, the bloodied bodies of his two lion guards were splayed on the ground in front of him. The tent itself had been destroyed, and tongues of flame still licked at the remnants.

Bean stood in stunned silence, his mind encompassed by the fog of death and destruction. The full enormity of the gruesome scene was unfolding before him. As far as he could see, the silhouettes of dead animals and humans covered the ground, the moon and firelight casting an ominous and deranged glow on their bodies. The night was alive with a constant chorus of anguished cries and screams of those that hadn't yet succumbed to their injuries. Having nowhere else to go, he began to make his way towards the dwelling of the meek and lowly one.

To his surprise, the small structure had not been destroyed and still looked to be in good condition. Approaching the entrance, Bean carefully pulled back the covering at the door. The inside of the dwelling was empty and quiet. In the middle of the room was a large table covered with five white linens. In the dim light, Bean quickly came to the ghastly realization that the linens were covering what he knew were dead bodies.

He stepped into the room and cautiously approached the table, gazing at the forms under the linens for what seemed an eternity, hesitating to do what he knew he must. Finally, summoning all of his courage, he reached down and pulled back the first covering. Immediately he recognized the face of Joshua. He jumped back, instinctively pulling the sheet back over Joshua's head. Tears began to well up in his eyes. He sank against the wall of the dwelling for several minutes, sobbing. Joshua had become a father to him in his short time in the Garden. He did not get to meet his real father, but he imagined him to be just like Joshua... and now he was gone.

Slowly regaining himself, he knew he must look at the other bodies. He would sooner die than do so, but he forced himself to his feet and neared the second body. He pulled back the cloth unveiling Seven's face. He put his hand to his mouth in horror, but he did not put the cloth back over her. He gently reached down and stroked her hair, muttering Seven's name over and over. Finally, he kissed her forehead softly and turned to the next body.

Before uncovering it, he knew by the shape of the figure under the linen it was Wart. When he pulled back the sheet, he fell on top of Warren's body, wailing in sorrow. He could only scream, "I'm sorry," again and again. The bitter knowledge he was the reason Wart was dead stabbed at his heart. He knew he would never be able to forgive himself. Even if he could return back home, how could he ever face his parents again?

After several minutes, he felt compelled to complete his gruesome task and uncover the remaining bodies. Pulling back the next sheet, he was puzzled. It was the face of a woman. At first he did not recognize her, but as the glow of the small lamp in the room danced on her face, he knew it was the woman that had visited him - he knew it was his mother.

Again he was brought to tears. He knew now he would never be able to speak with her or know her embrace.

Finally, Bean mustered a last ounce of courage to uncover the final body. Amidst his overwhelming grief and despair, he now felt a tinge of curiosity as he realized everyone he knew and truly cared about in this place was already lying before him on the table. He reached to remove the final linen, taking some small comfort in knowing that whoever it was under the sheet, it couldn't bring him any more heartache than he was then experiencing. He was wrong. Pulling back the sheet and resting it upon her chest, he staggered away in disbelief. Before him lay the lifeless body of his sister Katherine.

Chapter 20
Surrender

In the darkness, Bean sat up sharply, sweat dripping into his eyes. What did it all mean? He knew deep within him it was so much more than a nightmare. And what of his sister Katherine? Did the vision mean that somehow she was here in Edinnu? Was she in danger?

He sat for a time pondering the meaning of it all. The longer he thought, the more he could not escape the truth of the experience, dream or not. The scenes of devastation that were laid before him would most surely come to pass, and it was painfully clear to him at least some of his friends, possibly even Wart, would be killed in a battle with the forces of One.

With this understanding came a realization of what he must now do. He simply could not let it happen, even if it meant sacrificing his own life to stop it. To his surprise, the decision came easily and with certainty, as the thought of living with any other alternative was a fate he considered to be far worse than death. So, upon resolving firmly upon this new course of action, he quickly proceeded to dress and pack his few belongings. He carefully tucked the key stone under his pillow and hurriedly scrawled a note that read, *Please use this to get Warren back home.*

He quietly slid under the back of the tent and began to slowly move away from where his two guards were positioned. Such a task would have been more difficult two weeks ago, but part of Seven's training included a crash course on how to move stealthily and avoid detection. He wasn't great at it yet, but neither lion moved a muscle as he silently disappeared into the darkness towards the direction of the forest.

The six-hour journey was fairly uneventful in the darkness of the night. Bean did his best to avoid coming into contact with anyone along the way, but when he did cross paths with a human or animal, they did not seem to know who he was, nor did they question what he was doing there.

As the sun slowly began to light the morning sky, he neared the forest. With the dawn came a realization it would be a much more difficult task than he had anticipated getting past the True Believers' first line of defense, which had been established to repel the initial attack from One's forces. Surely he would be recognized as he made his way through the thousands of animals and humans preparing for the imminent battle.

Stumbling across a line of helmets on the ground, he picked one up and quickly put it on in hopes of disguising himself. He made his way from group to group until he finally arrived at the front line of the army. Satisfied with his efforts in reaching this point, he looked from side to side and realized he was now standing not more than ten feet from Joshua himself! Joshua's eyes were focused forward scanning the tree line, and Bean quickly moved backward and away before he could be detected. He kept moving down the line for a mile or so until the True Believer forces became more sparse and, eventually, he was alone.

He paused for a moment, trying to build up the courage to make his way across the neutral zone that separated the two armies. Even though the sun was now fully ablaze, there was a darkness to the tree line that gave him a moment of hesitation. He could only imagine the horrors that awaited him in that blackness.

Just as he worked up enough nerve to take his first step, a voice from behind him froze him in his tracks.

"And just where do you think you are going?"

Bean, initially startled, quickly realized the voice was Seven Hunter's. He turned around to see her standing behind him, pointing her arm directly at his heart.

"I knew you would try something like this," she said angrily.

Bean, looking at the barb pointed at his chest replied with a hint of amusement, "That's a little extreme isn't it? I thought we were friends."

"A friend wouldn't leave without saying goodbye," she retorted.

"Look, I'm just giving you what you wanted all along. You, above all people know how this will end if we go to war. If I give myself up, things can go back to the way they were."

"I never wanted to see you get killed," she replied with ferocity. "I've already risked my life for you. Don't you think I would gladly do it again?"

"I know you would, everyone here would. That's why I must do this. That's why I can't let it happen - not because of me."

"Well, it's not your decision to make. I'm not going to let you throw your life away. Not after all we've been through. Let's go, right now!" she ordered.

Bean looked at her for a moment. While he would never admit it to Seven, he had long ago fallen madly in love with her. He knew she could not have the same feelings for him, as he was so much younger, but that didn't lessen his affections. He felt there wasn't a thing he wouldn't do for her... except one.

"I'm sorry Seven," he said softly, breaking her gaze and looking down at the ground. "This is something I have to do."

Bean turned again and began walking toward the tree line.

"Stop or I'll shoot," she yelled after him.

This brought a slight smile to Bean. He knew the last thing she would do was hurt him. She yelled again but this time with less conviction. Eventually, she lowered her bow in resignation and watched him as he slowly disappeared into the forest.

Chapter 21
One

arily entering the forest, Bean worked to quickly adjust his eyes to the darkness. Surprised to find himself alone, he looked back to see if he could still see Seven across the meadow. Turning again to the forest, he came face to face with two soldiers, each pointing a spear at his chest. Instinctively, he swung back around looking for an escape route, only to narrowly avoid impaling himself on the sharp silver tips of a Caretaker's antlers. Recognizing there was no way out for him now, he lowered his arms, closed his eyes and stood silently, awaiting his fate. Immediately a cloth sac was pulled over his head from behind, his arms pulled roughly behind his back and his wrists tied firmly together with rope.

Bean was jostled to and fro as he was pushed, pulled and dragged deep into the forest, further away from any hope of rescue - not that he wanted to be saved. He had made this decision to keep his friends out of danger, and any rescue attempt would surely result in failure and likely the death of those he was trying to protect. After an hour of trudging blindly through the forest, he was told to step up into what he surmised was some kind of carriage. A stern voice commanded him to sit and stay put. Bean obeyed and, as he sat, the carriage lurched forward towards an unknown destination. Although fully aware his situation was grim, he now felt a small sense of relief. Given his first encounter with the Caretakers in his world, he expected he would be killed immediately upon discovery. Every minute now was one he did not expect to have.

The carriage bumped along slowly for what seemed hours, though Bean found it difficult to measure the time with the sac still covering his head. Given the extended length of the journey, he found himself able to relax to a small degree. In an effort to avert his mind from what awaited him at the end of the trip, he found himself preoccupied with removing the cloth sac so he could try and regain some bearing of time and space. He began fidgeting to see if he could remove it without the use of his hands that remained securely tied behind his back.

"Would you like me to help you with that?" came a voice piercing the silence.

Startled, Bean sat up straight. It had been hours and, until now, he had presumed he was alone in the carriage. He had not heard a peep from anyone else for the entirety of the journey, nor had he heard any signs of life whatsoever.

Instinctively he blurted, "Who's there?"

"First things first," came the voice. "Let's remove this sac and unloose your restraints. I don't want it to get out that I am rude to my guests."

The man first untied the ropes around Bean's wrists and then slowly removed the covering over his head. He sat back opposite Bean in the carriage and stared curiously into his eyes.

The man was tall and thin, though he had a definite look of strength to him. His hair was a lustrous jet black, combed backward so it draped over his shoulders, ending just between his shoulder blades. He wore a long ivory coat that nearly reached the floor, with intricate stitching and embroidery that seemed at odds with all of the clothing styles Bean had previously encountered in the Garden. His face had rigid, striking features that suggested a man in his early forties. Bean had to admit he was one of the more handsome men he'd ever encountered, possessing an undeniable movie star quality about him. His skin was pale, making his dark hair even more striking than it otherwise would have been. Strangely, there was a certain ashiness to his skin that made the man seem as if he hadn't bathed in quite some time, a look that was out of place with his otherwise impeccable grooming and style. He wore black boots that rose just to below his knees. Even from the sitting position, Bean could tell the man was at least six and a half feet tall and created an imposing figure in front of him in the small confines of the carriage.

The feature that most caught Bean's attention was the man's eyes. They were of pure black, dotted with flecks of amber like the smoldering embers of a fire, creating the eerie impression that his eyes were always watching Bean, as if he were a painting on a wall.

"Now, to answer your question, my name is One."

The man paused for a moment to examine Bean's reaction, which, given the circumstances, remained surprisingly subdued.

"Yes, yes, I imagine you've heard some dreadfully awful things about me. Comes with the territory I suppose. It seems no matter how much you try, some people just won't be helped. I trust that, notwithstanding your young age, you'll show the maturity sufficient to base your own determinations of my character upon our actual interaction rather than pure conjecture and rumor."

One spoke with an elaborate flair, speaking loudly and stressing every word with preciseness as if acting in a play.

"I'm afraid my enemies have created a simply monstrous depiction of me in order to stir the people to rebellion. A very unhappy circumstance to be sure... but unavoidable I suppose. Such is the price of being the Savior."

"Savior?" Bean responded almost involuntarily, surprised that One would use that word to describe himself.

"Yes, yes, I know that must sound awfully egotistical of me - calling myself that. But it is a role that I assure you I have accepted with the utmost grace and humility. You see, I have been given that most sacred calling of ensuring the salvation of all the inhabitants of my kingdom, whether they be man or animal. Yes, yes, it is inherent in all creatures to inevitably succumb to the many frailties and foibles of this mortal existence. And so, it is only through my guidance and rule that they can be assured of navigating the vicissitudes of this reality and avoiding damnation in the worlds to come. Yes, yes, for all intents and purposes, I am quite literally, their Savior."

One paused again, allowing his words time to sink in.

"My apologies for being so outspoken. I do get carried away at times. Yes, yes, I see this may be a bit much for our first encounter. Speaking of encounters, I don't believe I caught your name my child."

Bean hesitated for a moment, not wanting to reveal his true identity, then realized One knew exactly who he was and was only toying with him now.

He sat up and spoke as boldly as he could muster; "My name is Benjamin Greene, but I believe you know me better as Benjamin James."

Bean could detect the corner of One's mouth curl up in amusement.

"Yes, yes, I thought as much. Benjamin James," he repeated to himself. "So you are the boy that is to bring about my utter and complete destruction."

"I really don't know anything about that. I just want to go home. I have nothing against you - or anyone for that matter. If you'll just let me go home, I promise to never bother you again," Bean's tone devolving from boldness to begging.

One sat for a moment, seeming to legitimately consider Bean's appeal, then spoke with what appeared to be genuine empathy.

"Yes, yes, I can see that you are in quite a predicament. One that you most certainly did not bring upon yourself. I want you to know that if I could have my preference, we would sit down for a lovely meal, and then I would send you on your way back to where you came from. Yes, yes, I certainly am inclined to that course of action. Unfortunately - and again I tell you this is through no fault of your own - I find myself in quite a quandary. All this nonsense about a prophecy and such. And wouldn't you know it, it is just those kinds of things that can cause a lot of trouble for someone in my position. You, Benjamin, are, unfortunately for you, a symbol of hope, and I've discovered over the years that there is simply nothing more dangerous than hope. Yes, yes, it is not you that is dangerous my boy, to be sure, it is simply the *idea* of you. Please try and understand I am only doing what is in the best interest of the people. I am only trying to help them. And if they won't accept my help, unfortunately, at times, I must force them to accept it. As you might imagine, this approach may engender a bit of resentment among the people - biting the hands that feed them so to speak. Yes, yes, there are some that would like nothing more than to use you, in a most despicable way, to advance their own agendas. Again, unfortunately for you, I simply can't let that happen."

"So, where are you taking me? What are you going to do to me?" Bean asked timidly.

"Yes, yes, I'm pleased to say we are on our way to One City, the most beautiful city in all of my kingdom. Once we arrive, you will be pampered and receive the finest care that One City has to offer. And then, well... at the appointed hour, you will be taken up upon the City wall for all to see. It is there that I will unsheathe my knife - and plunge it into your heart."

The two sat in an awkward silence for a moment until One spoke, smiling.

"But let's not let that spoil our journey."

Chapter 22
Grand Order

One informed Bean the journey to One City would take two days. After learning his fate, Bean was less than keen on making small talk with One during the remainder of the journey. That did not stop the leader of the Grand Order from a never-ending verbal waterfall describing and extolling the many virtues of the kingdom he had created.

The trip was to take the unlikely pair through three of the Seven Cities. The first stop for Bean since being placed in the carriage was Five City. As in Seven City, the homes were identical and the streets and blocks were laid out in a comparable configuration. Notwithstanding the similarities, it was clear the accommodations in Five City, though still meager, were markedly superior to those that Joshua and Seven had inhabited.

Only an eerie desolation inhabited the streets as the procession moved forward, but Bean noted virtually every home had at least one pair of eyes peering out through the small window to the right of each dwelling door. The caravan eventually came to a stop within the City square. Though considerably larger, it was configured in the same fashion as in Seven City. In the center of the Plaza was an identical monument to One, though it appeared larger than the one in Seven City and was made of a granite-like material rather than the black polished coal.

Another notable difference was the presence of what Bean could only describe as a train station. It was here he and One left the carriage and boarded a lavish riding car. The "train" itself consisted of three attached cars that were rounded in shape and much different in appearance than the box-cars he had become accustom to in his world. The pair boarded the middle car, which was larger and considerably more ornate than the two on either side. The cars in front and behind held eight archers perched back to back on a small platform on the roof, while two or three Caretakers rode inside with their heads and antlers sticking out the windows. The train itself ran on one large metal rail that rose above the ground three to four feet. The four wheels on each car attached horizontally to either side of the rail while the top of the rail was lined with what appeared to be ball bearings upon which the train cars glided along.

Once the group was settled, the cars lurched forward as an enormous plume of black smoke rose from beneath the first car, almost choking Bean as it permeated the air around him. One either did not notice the smoke or ignored it altogether, and shortly it dissipated.

The interior of the car was decidedly luxurious, though slightly dated and worn, reminding Bean of his Grandmother's house, full of knick-knacks and bobbles and lined and filled with ornate blankets, pillows, and curtains. Overall it had the general feel of someone making a considerable effort to try and make something that was slightly aged and tattered into something elegant and lavish.

One seemed to be sincerely enjoying Bean's company, notwithstanding the fact that he didn't speak but more than a few words to One over the course of their two day journey. Bean eventually determined it wasn't so much his company that One enjoyed, but rather One relished the opportunity to explain to an "outsider" what he had accomplished in the Grand Order and to shower praise upon his own efforts.

Over the course of their voyage, One laid out, in intricate detail, the manner in which he had come to power some twenty years earlier, rather matter-of-factly recounting the story of how he was forced to kill his father and older brother to become "One."

"Yes, yes, it was either them or me," he stated without a hint of emotion or regret. "It was for the good of the Grand Order really. Unfortunately, my father did not have the vision nor force of will necessary to effectively lead the people. And my brother, well, don't get me started on him."

One's preferred topic of conversation was imparting his particular philosophical view on the proper governance of his people, and he seemed to make it his personal mission to bring Bean around to his way of thinking.

"Yes, yes, I know much about the land you come from... this 'America,'" One said with a shallow but confident air.

"The erroneous devotion to individual freedoms above the collective good is a tired and egocentric worldview, destined to be condemned to the dung hills of history. Your people naively and greedily cling to a belief in individual salvation. I know that salvation can only come through the Grand Order. While you selfishly strive to save yourselves, consumed with your pettiness and self-absorbed with your precious feelings and hopes, you allow others to be thoughtlessly cast by the wayside. Don't you see that no one need be lost?" One said with an elevated earnestness, leaning forward.

Bean, surprised at the unexpected show of emotion, could only shrug his shoulders in response. He rarely even watched the news, and trying to formulate a response to One's well-rehearsed, dogmatic tirade was no less daunting than debating Einstein about the Theory of Relatively. After a time, One again leaned back and resumed a more measured tone.

"Yes, yes, of course salvation for all comes at a price. But is it not far better to lose a few individual freedoms in order that all may be saved?"

Again, One's question hung uncomfortably in the air. Finally, feeling compelled to provide more than a shrug in response, Bean replied with as much disinterest as he could muster.

"I really don't know. I guess I haven't given it much thought. I do know that I'm not very interested in the Grand Order if it means that you are going to kill me because of it."

One laughed heartily, "Yes, yes, it's just that type of impudence and impertinence that has no place in the Grand Order."

One continued undaunted, explaining each person and city in the Grand Order had a specific role to play. At a young age, every citizen is run through a battery of tests to determine their natural talents and aptitudes. Children are then assigned a particular "calling" that best suits their abilities. At that point the children are taken from their mother and father and placed with a mentor in order to teach them and develop their particular capacities. Anticipating an objection from Bean on the practice of removing a child from its family, One quickly and forcibly stated, "Yes, yes, I know it may seem harsh to the uneducated, but you must understand the Grand Order *is* the family. We are all brothers and sisters. We are all mothers and fathers."

Bean also learned individual names were not given to citizens within the Grand Order and that each person was identified with a number along with the designation of their particular vocation. Children would initially receive the highest number available but would receive a lower number when someone in front of them died or if they did something that showed a certain devotion to the Grand Order.

"Seven Hunter," Bean whispered to himself.

Not only could a person advance within his or her own calling, but those that were particularly dedicated to the Grand Order could eventually move from one city to another. A resident of Three City who, as One put it, "put the needs of the many over the needs of the few," could advance to Two City.

"Of course," One said matter-of-factly, "promotions within one's calling or from one city to another come with their share of advantages and benefits. And if there are those that fail to put the Grand Order first, well, they naturally receive a 'subtraction.' Too many subtractions are dealt with quite harshly, I'm afraid. Although I find it rare to have to use such discipline among my people, it is a necessary evil to motivate others to avoid making similar mistakes."

As the sky began to orange from the setting sun, the train pulled into the main square of Three City. Although the buildings in the main squares of both Seven City and Five City were ornate and impressive, it was immediately evident to Bean that Three City was a substantial step up. The obelisk in the center of the square was significantly larger than those he had previously encountered and was comprised of what Bean could only guess was pure gold. Gazing upon the sparkling tower, he realized he was looking upon something worth literally hundreds of millions of dollars, yet there were no guards... well, none that he could see anyway.

Bean was led to a beautiful two story building on the east side of the square that appeared to function as the home of Three City's "One Governor," who had just hastily emerged from the mansion to greet One, frantically tucking in his shirt as he approached Bean's group. It seemed One's visit had taken the man completely by surprise, and he was clearly flustered and unnerved by the unannounced visit from the leader of the Grand Order. The man knelt on the ground in front of One, who simply walked past him without any kind of acknowledgement.

Almost forgetting his travelling companion, One stopped in the doorway and turned to Bean, saying, as almost an afterthought, "Yes, yes, a most enjoyable day indeed. I look forward to tomorrow."

With that One entered the mansion, the door slamming loudly behind him. Immediately, Bean felt a sharp poke in his back. He turned to see the silver pointed horns of a Caretaker immediately behind him.

"Let's move," it said gruffly, directing Bean to that same part of the square where the jail was located in Seven City.

It was clear the building now before him was also a jail, but significantly more fortified than the one in which he had previously been imprisoned. No doubt One had been fully apprised of his escape there, and was determined Bean not have a similar opportunity here. He was placed in a cell and a Caretaker, its right eye socket scarred and missing an eyeball, stood facing him, its one good eye glued to his every movement. Bean surmised it would be stationed there for the entirety of the night, and he imagined it would be difficult to sleep with that single red eye boring into his back.

The Caretaker spoke, "What of my brothers?"

The question took Bean off guard, and he furrowed his brow not fully understanding the question.

"What of my brothers?" the Caretaker asked again, this time more forcefully.

Bean started, "I'm not sure what you..."

"You know exactly what I mean," it said angrily, stomping its front hoof onto the stone floor. "What happened to the two Caretakers that were sent into your world?"

Bean paled, well-knowing that at least one, and likely both, were dead. Considering it the wiser course of action, he feigned ignorance.

"Honestly, I don't know what you're talking about," he responded, trying his best to sound convincing under the frightening, singular gaze of the animal.

The Caretaker sprang forward, crashing its antlers into the bars of the cell.

"If I find out that anything has happened to them, I'll make you pay. And if that happens, you will beg for One to kill you."

Bean slowly lay down, turning his back to the Caretaker, the cell bars still ringing from the impact of the silver antlers. He laid his head on the pillow thinking he would never fall asleep, but the events of the day had taken more of a toll than he had supposed and, in seconds, he was slumbering.

Bean was awoken early in the morning, given a small breakfast, and led back to the train car where One was already waiting.

"Yes, yes, good morning Benjamin James," One said cheerily. "A big day indeed. I can't wait for you to see One City. It is really something to behold!"

"I'm sure it is," Bean replied with more than a hint of sarcasm.

The train plunged into the lush vegetation of the forest towards its final destination. Bean stared out the window in an attempt to distract himself from One's renewed chatter. Losing himself in the never ending greenery passing before him, a distinct flash of red suddenly caught his eye halfway up an approaching tree. Upon closer inspection, Bean saw it was an arrow stuck into the tree trunk with a small red square piece of cloth attached to its shaft. He could tell something was written on the cloth but couldn't quite make it out at first. He strained to read it as the train rushed by and saw that a single number was written on the fabric - the number 7.

Chapter 23
Happiness

"Could that possibly be Seven's arrow?" thought Bean anxiously to himself as the train continued on towards One City. If it was, how could she have traveled so quickly? Except for their overnight stop in Three City, his group had been traveling non-stop since his capture. With her knowledge of the Seven Cities and her skills as a hunter, Seven would certainly be able to make up a lot of ground, but, even so, she would need to travel through the night, without any rest, to have any hope of catching them. And what did it mean? If it was Seven, there was no doubt she would make some attempt to free him. This gave Bean a flash of hope that was immediately doused with the realization that any such attempt would likely result in not only his death, but the death of Seven. He had left to protect her, and if it was indeed her arrow, she was now in more danger than ever.

In an effort to distract himself from such awful thoughts, he decided to break his self-imposed silence and ask One a question.

"I've met some of the people in your Grand Order, and they don't seem to be very happy. What good is being saved if you're not happy?"

"Well, well, he speaks!" said One affecting surprise. "Yes, yes, and a most insightful question from such a young boy. First of all, let me state unequivocally that happiness is completely and utterly overrated. If we are to be completely honest with ourselves, no one is ever truly happy. But, I am not one to avoid a question. So, let me begin my answer to your question with one of my own. In your world, do your parents allow you to do whatever you wish to do?"

"Well... no," Bean conceded grudgingly.

"Yes, yes, of course not. I'm sure you'd agree any parent that let their child do anything they wanted would be acting irresponsibly at best. And why do you think parents do not let their children do whatever they want?"

Bean thought for a moment, "Because their parents know what's best for them?"

"Quite right again, my child. Yes, yes, you are a bright one to be sure. Parents give their children rules, provide them duties, teach them discipline and require them do those things they know will be in their best interest."

"I suppose," mumbled Bean, sensing he was being beaten.

"You suppose correctly. And does your parents' forcing you to do these things make you happy?"

"Not really," Bean said in resignation.

"Yes, yes, quite miserable I'm supposing. And what possible reason could parents have for doing things that make their children unhappy?"

Bean grumbled, "Because they love them and want them to do what's right."

"Yes, yes, my son. And that is exactly what I am doing for those in the Grand Order. I love my people. I am simply giving them rules and responsibilities, teaching them discipline, and ensuring they make the right decisions. To be sure, this may make them unhappy at times in this life, but it will guarantee their happiness in their lives to come. Do you not think it is best to endure a few moments of unhappiness now, to gain an eternity of joy?"

"Why can't people be happy now *and* have an eternity of joy?" Bean shot back.

"By happiness, I can only assume that you mean freedom, or more particularly freedom to choose, the most tired and irksome argument of them all. Why, I can't seem to have one conversation with your ilk without hearing how wonderful and essential free agency is. And what does freedom to choose get you? I'll tell you what it gets you - heartbreak and sorrow. Yes, yes, I suppose there are a small few like myself that can be trusted to make correct decisions for themselves, but it is clear that any man, or animal for that matter, left to their own devices, will eventually make the wrong decisions. Decisions that will ultimately and inevitably lead to their downfall. Your God tells you to be perfect, does He not? Ha, a sheer impossibility on its face. It is man's nature to inescapably succumb to the carnal and base desires that so easily and often befall him. Why, if left to himself, he will devolve into the basest of creatures, seeking only to satisfy the lusts of the flesh. So your loving God pretends to care for His children, but then does nothing to ensure their salvation. In fact, He does quite the opposite. By His very actions He condemns them. Would your parents be so cruel and uncaring? No, they lead you by the hand, helping you make correct choices and disciplining you when you don't. The fact is, people cannot be trusted with matters as important as their very salvation. When left to their own designs, they will certainly and undoubtedly fail."

One paused for a moment to see if his words were having their intended effect before continuing.

"Why, look at your so called friends. They lounge and laze all day 'tending to the Garden.' Where does that get them? No doubt they claim they are happy, but what do they have to show for it? Pretty flowers? Then look at what the Grand Order has accomplished. Seven magnificent cities to rival any in your world, all serving the whole. Everyone's needs are met. No one goes hungry. No one is lost. Everyone contributes. They have purpose. They are not left alone. That, my boy, is paradise, not the Garden."

Bean knew he was no match to argue the matter with One. After a few moments, he defiantly shouted in desperation the only thing he could think to say.

"I think there is nothing more important than being happy!"

For a brief moment, the smoldering embers in One's eyes erupted into a hot rage as he leaned forward and raised his right hand as if to strike Bean across the face. Catching himself, One quickly regained his composure and leaned back as if entirely undisturbed by Bean's audacity.

"Yes, yes, I suppose I have given you more credit than you deserved. It is difficult to argue reason when your opponent's reality is based in pure fantasy. A fruitless endeavor in any case, given your imminent fate. Yes, yes, quite literally a waste of breath on my part, given what little breath you have left in you."

Bean turned and again looked out the window. He could just make out the outline of a large city on the horizon.

Chapter 24
Ice Cream Cones

One City lay at the base of a large, rounded hill. The outskirts were similar to the others Bean had encountered in Edinnu, but the size and quality of the homes and other buildings were strikingly improved. The streets were paved with a material that sparkled slightly in the sunlight, giving the roads the appearance of having been soaked by a recent rainstorm. In contrast to the other cities, One City was bustling with activity, as people rushed to and fro like so many bees in a hive. The train cars paused momentarily as they approached the City center. Bean looked out of the window to see a massive wall, at least fifty feet high and made of thick grey stone, surrounding the heart of the City. A large iron gate was quickly opened allowing the train cars to pass through and, in just a few moments, the small caravan reached what was to be its final destination, the main plaza of One City.

"Well," One began, awkwardly touching Bean on his knee, "this is where we part ways. Yes, yes, I have very much enjoyed our brief time together. I'm afraid our next meeting will not be so pleasant. I do apologize for that. I hope there are no hard feelings on your part. As it is, please try and enjoy your last day. Yes, yes, if there is anything you want, need or desire, please don't hesitate to ask."

With that, One started to rise and, not quite knowing the best way to bid farewell to his traveling companion, clumsily patted him on the head and hurriedly left the carriage, leaving Bean to himself.

Soon after, a small knock came on the train car door as it slowly opened, revealing a small elderly gentleman.

"Allow me to introduce myself, I am One Majordomo," the old man said, slightly bowing. "I will be at your service during your stay here. If you'll follow me, I'll show you to your accommodations."

Stepping out of the train car, Bean shielded his eyes from the rays of sunlight ricocheting off the sleek, metallic exteriors of the massive buildings that now surrounded him. Again, in the center of the square was positioned the obelisk, but standing three to four times the size of the others he had previously encountered in the Grand Order. The monument appeared to consist of silver or platinum. At the time, Bean could hardly imagine a more beautiful structure than the gold obelisk in Three City, but the sun reflecting off of the silver towering column before him held him utterly transfixed. Most of the buildings in the square were topped with large spires that formed a kaleidoscope of colors and shapes. The most impressive was a large stone edifice located at the base of the hill with eight massive columns lining the front entrance and colossal gold inlaid scenes in bas-relief along the top and sides. Behind the columns was a large golden door that was just now opening to permit One's entry.

One's palace, thought Bean.

The hill itself rose up directly behind the palatial structure. Radically different from any of the other landscapes Bean had previously encountered in Edinnu, it immediately caught his eye. The hill was sunburned and barren and appeared to be completely uninhabited and devoid of any vegetation except for a lone, dead, spindly tree located at the summit. It appeared the only approach to the hill itself was through the palace, as a large wall lined the entirety of the hill's circumference and attached to either side of the fortress. Taking in the full scene again, it was clear to Bean that one of the primary functions of the palace was to serve as a large gateway to access the hill.

"If you'll follow me, sir," repeated One Majordomo, diverting Bean's attention away from the hill.

He turned, following the small man to a building on the side of the Plaza that was in closest proximity to the palace. One Majordomo was dressed in a long black robe and, Bean thought, was a hundred year's old if a day. The top of his head was completely bald, but from the base of his skull protruded a long, rope-like braid of grey hair that almost touched the back of his knees. He could hardly takes his eyes off it as it swung back and forth in almost perfect time as the man walked in front of him.

The duo were now the sole inhabitants of the massive plaza as the soldiers and Caretakers that accompanied Bean and One on their journey removed themselves once One had safely entered the palace. However, a casual examination of his surroundings revealed a soldier stationed every ten feet or so on top of the surrounding wall. Bean also noted the one-eyed Caretaker that stood guard over him the night before was now standing next to the main plaza gate, its eye never straying from Bean's person. Escape, if any, would most certainly not come via that particular exit. The door closing behind him and One Majordomo, Bean shivered, glad to be free of the Caretaker's gaze.

Bean trudged up four flights of stairs, following the old man to the top floor of the building.

"I trust you'll enjoy these accommodations," One Majordomo said, as he opened the door and motioned for Bean to enter. The room itself was enormous, comprising the entirety of the top story. Grandiose and imposing paintings with ornate golden frames adorned the walls, most including some dramatic representation of One in various acts of valor or heroism. A large marble balcony opened out onto the Plaza. Stepping into the sunlight, Bean quickly noted it was far too high to hope for any escape. Further discouraging any remaining hope of freedom was the unmistakable weight of hundreds of invisible eyes surveying his every movement.

"I've taken the liberty of arranging some of our finest delicacies for your enjoyment," said One Majordomo, motioning to a table in the corner of the room overflowing with different kinds of cuisine.

Bean felt his stomach lurch at the sight and smell of the food, and he realized he hadn't eaten since that morning. Rushing to the table, he grabbed what appeared to be the leg of a large game bird. He eagerly brought it to his lips but, just as he was about to sink his teeth into the meat, he abruptly stopped himself. During his two weeks in the Garden, he had met so many different kinds of animals and never ceased to be amazed that they could actually think and talk. He sat astonished and entertained as he listened to their many tales and legends. He loved how each animal possessed a distinct, and often humorous, way of thinking and speaking. He was moved by the profound ideas and feelings they expressed and was touched by the depth and devotion each exhibited towards their families and friends. Looking at the piece of meat in his hands, he realized this bird had come from Edinnu. Immediately his stomach turned as he understood that if he consumed what he now held in his hand, it would be the same as eating one of his new, magnificent friends.

"Is there something the matter?" asked the old man.

Bean slowly laid the drumstick back on the table.

"I think I'll pass on the meat, if it's all the same to you."

"Certainly sir, eat as much or as little as you like. If there is anything else you should desire, please press this," One Majordomo said pointing at a small button on the wall, "and I will do my best to accommodate you. Anything at all, just press the button."

With that One Majordomo quietly and quickly exited the room, leaving Bean to himself.

He prepared a plate of fruit and pastry from the table and plopped himself on a large red sofa in the center of the room. The couch was like quicksand, the soft cushions giving way to Bean's backside. His furniture back home seemed to be made out of cement in comparison. Wriggling his body to adjust for the supple sofa, he began to eat and, after a time, began a detailed examination of each painting on the wall before him. The largest painting, hung directly in front of him, was of One in the midst of a great and terrible battle. His foot was rested on the head of a dead lion while his hand held a large sword triumphantly in the air. Most of the other paintings were in a similar vein. Knowing that One was looking down on him from every conceivable angle, Bean began to fidget uncomfortably, sinking even deeper into the sofa.

Bean's eye was eventually drawn to a small painting hidden away in a corner hallway off of the main room. Notwithstanding its minimal size, the picture stood out for its uniqueness in comparison to all of the other paintings, if for no other reason than One was not the central focus. He extricated himself from his seat to investigate the picture in greater detail. It had a simple wooden frame that appeared to be handmade, a stark contrast from the gilded, decorative frames that surrounded the other paintings

He neared the painting and saw its main subject was a tree that appeared to have a variety of colorful fruit hanging from its branches. Although he now found himself standing directly in front of the painting, he could not yet discern exactly what kind of tree it was, given the small size of the painting and the peculiar shape of the fruit. He leaned in closer so his nose was almost touching the canvas. He stopped breathing for a moment. Those weren't fruit hanging on the tree at all - they were lollipops!

Bean rushed to the wall, frantically pushing the button until One Majordomo re-entered the room.

"How can I be of service to you, sir?"

Bean hurriedly ushered him to the hallway where the painting was hung.

"Can you tell me please," he said trying to catch his breath, "who painted this picture?"

"Why, I believe that was painted by one of the Ladies in Waiting... number four if I recall correctly."

"I must see her! Can you bring her to me?" Bean implored, almost bursting with excitement.

"I'm afraid that is quite impossible. I have been given strict instruction that you are neither to see, nor be seen by, anyone."

"Please, please, it is urgent that I see her. It will only take a moment," Bean pleaded.

"I'm sorry, but if I allowed it, I could be killed. It is an impossible thing you ask of me," One Majordomo replied with what appeared to be sincere regret.

Bean flung himself on the couch and burst into tears. He had wondered for so long what had happened to Katherine, and now he was sure he had found her. It simply had to be her. She was here in One City, likely within this very Plaza, and now he could not see her or speak to her. He would be killed in the morning and would never have the chance to be with her again, even if only for a moment. It was more than he could bear and, no longer able to contain himself, he buried his head into the nearest pillow and began screaming and kicking violently.

One Majordomo, trying to make some sense of the sudden outburst, sat gently next to Bean on the couch and, patting him on the back, asked, "Do you know this woman?"

Bean arrested his sobbing for a moment, suddenly realizing the danger he was placing Katherine in. If he told One Majordomo she was his sister, he would likely report it to One and, if that happened, he may not be the only one that would be executed in the morning.

One Majordomo, sensing Bean's hesitation to divulge any information, offered, "Yes, I remember Four Lady in Waiting. She is a very kind and beautiful woman. I swear to you that I will not do anything that will jeopardize her safety."

Peeking over his pillow at One Majordomo, Bean could see the genuineness in his eyes, but still couldn't bring himself to reveal she was his sister. After all, as kind as he seemed, One Majordomo must have exhibited great loyalty to One in the past to have earned his lofty position.

"Well..." he began cautiously, "I'm not quite sure if it is her, but she may be an acquaintance from my past that I have not seen in many years. As this is my last day, I was hoping to see a familiar face before, well, you know," Bean said trying to sound convincing.

One Majordomo paused for a moment in thought.

"I'm afraid there is no way for you to see her... there is no getting around that. I suppose if you wanted to give her a message,

I could try and get it to her, but I cannot make any promises. It would have to be very short and something that, if found, could not be traced back to you."

"Oh thank you, thank you so much," Bean gushed as he reached for a pen and paper that were on the nearby desk. He placed the end of the pen in his mouth as he did when trying to answer a difficult math question in school... and then, a wry smile crossed his face as he busily began drawing a picture. When he was finished, One Majordomo examined the drawing.

"What is it? I've never seen anything like it."

Bean replied, "Oh, it's nothing really. Just an ice cream cone."

Chapter 25
The Vision

Staring at the ceiling from his massive, down-filled, four posted bed, Bean quickly realized sleep would remain elusive for the indefinite future. He rose and walked out onto the balcony, gazing across the Plaza and over the wall into the vast expanse of city and forest. One City itself was dark, dotted only with the light of a few lamps and torches burning across the massive breadth of the capital. Bean guessed no one from Edinnu had been to his world for several hundreds of years, as electricity did not seem to be available, or even to exist, here. Remembering as best he could the pictures from his history books at school, the surroundings seemed most to reflect the trappings of 16th or 17th century Europe. That may have been the last time anyone in Edinnu had any significant contact with his world... except of course, for him and his mother.

Staring into the darkness, he knew Seven was likely somewhere near and she would inevitably attempt some strategy to free him, which thought brought him great anxiety and distress. He knew any element of surprise had been lost long ago, and One was waiting to snap like a hungry crocodile at just such an attempt. He also knew any bid to escape would certainly be futile and would likely result in Seven's death. Even if he were to escape, he would be back to the original position he found himself in at the Garden, putting not just Seven's life in danger, but thousands and thousands of the True Believers.

Given the shocking revelation earlier that day, his mind could not stray far from thoughts of his sister. Bean's mind was aflutter with questions. How could she have made it here? Did One take her from his home in Missouri? If One did take her, why was he left behind? What would One want with Katherine anyway? As far as he knew, she had no connection to the Garden - or One - or any of this. Maybe, like him, she had found this place by accident. But how did she end up in One's court in the middle of One City? He so longed to see her and to be with her again. He ached to tell his parents she was still alive. It would make them so happy.

His parents... oh how he missed them. He would give anything just to see them once more, only now fully realizing how much he had taken their love and support for granted. His heart's only desire was to see them again and tell them how sorry he was. Imagining how difficult these last few weeks must have been for them since he and Wart entered Edinnu caused his chest to tighten. There was no way for them to know what happened. He had experienced first-hand how much losing his sister wounded their souls. Now all of their children would have disappeared without any explanation. How could they bear it? Bean grasped the railing, steadying himself from the weight of his thoughts.

And what of Wart? After tomorrow, would he be able to get back to their parents in Missouri? Would he be able to tell them what had happened and at least give them some answers? He knew Joshua and the meek and lowly one would do everything within their power to return Wart to his home - but there was no guarantee. He wished he could see his little brother a final time and tell him he loved him, and that he was sorry for not being a better big brother.

Finally, amidst the flood of thoughts and emotions, Bean's mind rested upon his own mortality. He knew that tomorrow... he would die. He had originally thought he would be killed when he turned himself over to One in the forest, but then there was little time to contemplate death itself. Now, all alone in the middle of the night, there was nothing but time to think. Would it hurt? What would happen to him when he died? Would that be the end of him... or, was there more? His parents believed in God and in heaven and he dutifully went to church every Sunday, but, if he were to be truthful, his attendance was not out of any particular devotion. He went mostly because his parents wanted him to go, and it was what was expected. Not that he didn't believe, just that he had never developed any significant feelings either way. Church was simply something he did, not something to believe in. The fact was, he hadn't been forced to really consider the matter until now... now that it was too late. But, Bean rationalized, if there was a God, maybe He could save him. At the very least, he reasoned, maybe God could watch over his family and friends after he was gone. He concluded that it couldn't do any harm to pray.

Bean knelt down on the balcony and whispered the first sincere prayer of his life.

"Dear God, if you can hear me, please be with my Mother and Father and watch over them and comfort them. Please let them know that I love them. Please help my sister Katherine and my brother Warren to return home. Please watch over Seven and Joshua. Please tell them not to try and save me."

He paused for a moment as tears began to force their way through his closed eyes.

"I'm sorry I have not been a better person. I know deep inside that I could be better. I'm sorry I wasn't kinder. I'm sorry I wasn't more faithful. I'm sorry I wasn't a better... son. If I am before you tomorrow, I hope you will forgive me."

As Bean uttered the word, Amen, the whistle of a small bird penetrated the stillness of the night. He knew the sound immediately - it was Maximus! Springing to his feet, he peered into the darkness toward the direction of the noise. Seeing only blackness, he whispered, "Maximus."

No response.

"Maximus," he whispered louder, "I'm here." Still nothing.

Searching the night for his friend, he suddenly noticed a small light materialize on top of the barren hill behind the palace. The light grew until, in just a few seconds, he had to shield his eyes from the brightness. Adjusting to the intensity, he could see the tree on top of the hill, but it was markedly different from the one he had seen earlier in the day. It was now a large, beautiful, vibrant tree. Its color was pure white, surpassing anything he had ever before beheld. Even from this considerable distance, he could clearly make out the fruit of the tree hanging from the branches. The fruit gave off a luminescent golden glow and he immediately wanted nothing more than to taste it. The intense light seemed to emanate from within the tree itself, radiant beams shooting from the tips of its branches like small bolts of lightning. The magnificent splendor of the tree lit the night sky as if it were midday. The entirety of the picture before him was far beyond anything he had ever witnessed before. His mouth opened slightly as he beheld the wonder and majesty of the scene now unfolding before him.

His attention was drawn to what appeared to be three beings standing directly in front of the tree, each dressed in robes matching its brightness. He assumed the beings were women as each had long, flowing, bright red hair that seemed to be made of fire. The three women formed a semicircle near the front of the tree and stood with their heads bowed and their hands pressed together in front of their faces, as if in prayer.

A magnificently brilliant rod of fire, measuring five or six feet long, rotated between the tree and the women. Bean stared hypnotically at the movement of the rod that seemed to be handled by some invisible swordsman.

Almost as abruptly as the vision appeared before Bean, it vanished... the light fading, and the hill resuming its former barren appearance. The tree reverted to its previous lifeless form, its dead, barren branches now reflecting in the light of the moon.

Bean collapsed into a nearby chair as fatigue overwhelmed him. The experience couldn't have lasted for more than a few seconds, yet his entire body felt drained of every last ounce of energy. After a short while, he regained a degree of strength and managed to make his way back into bed.

Was this vision some kind of answer to his prayer? He couldn't be sure. But he now found his mind clear of the sadness, fear and anxiety that had enveloped him just moments earlier and, in a few moments, he was asleep.

Chapter 26
Execution Day

The morning brought the first cloudy day Bean could recall during his time in Edinnu. He assumed it must rain in this place, given the overabundance of flora around him, but nary a drop had fallen since his arrival. Such were the accidental thoughts that drifted in and out of Bean's mind as he stood on the top of the wall looking out on to One City. Brought there in the early morning hours, he had now been standing in the same spot for some time, surrounded by what he considered a ridiculous number of guards. He knew full well that one guard would be sufficient to stop him from escaping, but One was clearly taking no chances today. Bean had been awoken by the same bell he'd heard previously in Seven City, summoning all citizens within its reach to the main plaza. This time, it pealed out a constant cacophony until he was brought to the top of the wall, then mercifully, it came to a stop.

Bean looked beyond the tens of thousands of people now gathered below him. In the distance, to the side of the hill, a colossal river gradually split off into four separate rivers, each disappearing at various points in the horizon. The headwaters seemed to emerge directly from behind the hill itself. His home in Missouri was within a few hundred miles of the Mississippi River and he'd seen it a time or two, but each of the four individual rivers dwarfed it in both size and volume. He could see the water was crystal clear, even at this distance, and the massive flow sparkled with what little sunlight was able to break through the overcast skies.

Bean's attention jarred back to the reality of his current predicament when a commotion arose from within a guard house a few hundred feet to the left of his position. The large wooden door swung open and several men and women in brightly colored attire emerged, followed by a group of twelve men dressed in bright red silk robes, marching in lock step two by two. Finally, One appeared, dressed in a brilliant purple robe lined with what appeared to be the hair from the mane of a lion. A group of thirty women, dressed entirely in white, trailed One, their faces and heads covered with thin veils. Together, the entire group created a cornucopia of color and pageantry that would make the Queen of England envious.

Simultaneous with One's appearance, a large cheer erupted from the crowd below. Bean gazed at the throng curiously. The cheers took him off guard, as his limited interaction with the people of the Grand Order did not suggest to him that they were particularly fond of One. Perhaps, he thought, given the improved conditions in One City, the citizenry were more inclined to be in a position of support than those in the lower numbered cities.

One seemed to revel in the applause and raised his arms as if to physically gather in the adoration from his followers. As he did so, the people began to shout in unison, "ALL PRAISE TO ONE! ALL PRAISE TO ONE!"

After drinking his fill of adulation, One turned his attention to Bean's location and began to make his way toward him. At certain designated points, those in front of One in the procession stopped, turned, and knelt as he continued on past them. Finally, One alone stood next to Bean and faced the crowd. Upon raising his hand, the applause and shouting immediately ceased. Bean was amazed that so many people could become so quiet so quickly.

One paused for several seconds, as if trying to build anticipation for his words. Finally, shouting in a booming voice that Bean imagined could be heard for miles, One began, "I present to you - the Deliverer!"

Again a huge roar erupted from the crowd. One nodded his head in approval, in no hurry to continue. Finally, he raised his hand, again producing immediate and utter silence.

"I present to you - the 'Prophet' who would destroy One!"

This time his words were met with a chorus of boos and jeers from below.

Quieting the crowd, One continued, "We shall see, we shall see."

One paused again, as if now in profound thought, then motioned towards the twelve men in red robes. Quickly, one of them holding a small box rose from his knees and proceeded hastily towards One. Bowing, he opened the box, offering up its contents. Bean could immediately see it contained a small dagger. He was at once sickened and intrigued by the knife, realizing instantly that, with this tool, One would end his life. Yet even with this unsettling awareness, he couldn't help but note the knife itself was of a very low quality. The blade was dirty and rusty with a simple wooden handle wrapped in a worn, cracked leather casing. Bean thought it odd that this was the tool the great One, who surrounded himself with such ornate and elegant things, would use to kill him.

One reached into the box, grabbed the dagger and turned to the crowd, raising it high in the air for everyone to see. The throng burst into a wild frenzy at the sight of the weapon. This time, One made no motion for them to stop. Instead he turned to Bean, put his arm around his shoulder and raised the knife in front of him.

One leaned in, his lips lightly brushing against Bean's ear, causing the hair on the back of Bean's neck to bristle.

"If you look closely, you can still see the blood of that first traitor who tried to steal Father Cain's birthright."

Though no Bible scholar, Bean had heard the story of Cain and Abel enough times to recognize the reference. His eyes widened, realizing in front of him now was the first murder weapon in the history of the world.

"I hope you realize what a great honor I am bestowing upon you by using this dagger to end your life," One said with the utmost sincerity, seemingly expecting a thank you from Bean.

With none forthcoming, One again quieted the crowd.

"Before I proceed to carry out my sacred duty today, I first wish to show my great benevolence by granting my young friend here one final kindness before I send him to that awful hell which most surely awaits him."

One now motioned to someone on Bean's right. Immediately the door on the opposite guard tower opened. The sun briefly broke through the cloud cover, forcing Bean to squint and rendering him unable to make out the person now being ushered toward him. When his eyes adjusted sufficiently, although he had never before seen her in person, he knew immediately it was his mother, Dawn. His heart jumped. Since his vision of the tree the night before, he had been strangely calm to this point in the proceedings, but, as his mother approached him, he became overwhelmed with anxiety and fear, not for himself - but for her.

Brought directly before them, she did not look at or acknowledge One, but instead focused her eyes intently on Bean's face. He had seen the same sad expression before; it was the look of despair in his mother's eyes when Katherine had vanished. And then, like a ray of sunshine piercing through the darkest of clouds, her face suddenly lightened as a large smile broke across her face.

Caressing his cheek tenderly with the back of her hand, she spoke, "All these many years I have dreamed of seeing you again. No day has gone by that I did not pray for you and think of you. You are more beautiful than I ever could have dreamed. My joy is full now, being with you again."

As she spoke, tears filled Bean's eyes.

"Mother, I..." he tried to speak but couldn't.

She gently hushed him, softly kissing him on the cheek, then brought him to her in an embrace. As she held him in her arms, she whispered, "I am so very sorry."

"Don't be sorry mother. I... I missed you too. I just didn't know it until now."

As Bean finished his words, he could feel her body suddenly tense and her embrace tighten. In a moment, it relaxed again, and she spoke gently, "Remember my son, the end of your journey is only the beginning."

She stepped back and looked again into his eyes. Bean had never felt such pure love and, for a time, he was lost in her gaze, the dire circumstances surrounding him vanishing in her smile. In the corner of her mouth, a small pool of blood began to form. Now, for the first time, Bean noticed One standing directly behind his mother. He spoke to Bean, his eyes now devoid of any light.

"I told you hope is dangerous. Unfortunately, you are not the only one that provides hope."

With that he pulled out the dagger from the back of Bean's mother.

"No!" Bean shrieked, lunging at One.

The guards on either side immediately restrained him, One cackling at the vain attempt. Bean's mother staggered backward, then sank to her knees. One reached down, grabbed her roughly by the neck, lifted her with one hand over the wall's edge - and dropped her lifeless body toward the crowd below.

Chapter 27
Futility

Bean's hands and feet were lashed to two nearby posts that appeared to have been constructed for that very purpose. The stone under him had been stained red from what Bean could only guess was blood from others that had met their demise at this very spot.

One leaned in again and whispered coldly, "Not to worry, you will be with your mother very shortly."

He turned to the crowd and again lifted the dagger, now dripping with the crimson blood of Bean's mother.

"The time has come to end the false prophecy that has brought so much death and destruction upon our land, and to prove to all everywhere that the god of Cain is more powerful than the god of Adam."

With that, One raised his arm and readied the dagger. Bean closed his eyes and, resigned to his fate, felt a renewed sense of peace. It would all be over in a moment.

"I am One. I am Power. I am Light and Truth. By my command, all things are governed. Through my hand, all mankind shall be saved. All kingdoms, power and glory to me," One roared as the dagger began its descent.

Before it could reach its intended mark, several guards stationed along the top of the wall yelled in unison, "Arrows!"

Upon hearing the shouts, One's hand veered away from Bean's chest. Instead he grabbed the hem of his robe, quickly wrapping himself in the purple cloth. Bean opened his eyes to see a quick succession of metal barbs glancing harmlessly off of the center of One's back and clinking against the stone at his feet, as if he was protected by some type of invisible force field. Silence rang over the crowd before a low chorus of murmurs broke out. When it was clear that no more arrows were imminent, One emerged from under the protection of his robe, sweeping his cloak in a grandiose circle above his head while spinning toward the crowd to unveil himself unscathed. A massive wave of cheers swept over the group on the wall. Bean looked in the direction of the arrows and saw that a large group of guards had now converged on a hooded shooter.

He knew before the guards revealed the culprit that it was Seven. Immediately thrust back into a state of panic and fear, he thought to himself, why couldn't she just let me die? At the same time, he knew Seven too well to think she would not make some attempt to save him. He had just watched his mother killed in front of him. Now he knew his best friend would die as well.

"Bring her to the wall," boomed One to the guards who had seized Seven.

She was dragged kicking and fighting through the throng to the base of the wall just as a long rope ending in a noose was lowered down. Seven's hands were tied behind her back and the noose placed around her neck.

Again Bean screamed "No!" to One as he futilely struggled to free himself from his bands. One turned, amused.

"Not to worry, I'm not going to kill her... at least not yet. I simply thought she may like a front row seat to the execution of the boy for whom she has so foolishly sacrificed her life."

A group of four guards pulled on the rope, and Seven began to be hauled up the side of the wall by her neck, spinning and bouncing helplessly against the stone. By the time she reached the top, the rope had worn her neck raw, and she was nearly unconscious. The guards quickly removed the noose and brought Seven stumbling and breathless towards One and Bean.

"Did you not think I would be prepared for your feeble attempt to free the boy? Your paltry missiles are no match for me," One laughed, almost giddy. "Are you impressed with my new robe?" he asked, whirling around for Seven and Bean to see. "I had it specially made for this very occasion. My gifted tailor came up with the fabric - fully arrow proof. Yes, yes, being in my position does indeed have its advantages."

He turned to Bean, shaking his head disappointedly.

"I must say though, I expected a little better from your friends. I mean really, one small girl is the best they could do? Perhaps they do not esteem you as highly as I had supposed. Yes, yes, I admit, I am a bit insulted on your behalf."

"Perhaps they assumed that one small girl was all it would take," shot Seven back at One, having regained her breath and her venom.

One laughed again, "If you weren't already dead, that comment would have certainly sealed your fate. As it is, perhaps a hanging would go a long way to quieting that impudent mouth of yours. Yes, yes, you've had a taste of the noose, and it would appear you are quite eager to finish the meal."

"It doesn't matter what you do to me," Seven yelled loud enough for the crowd to hear. "The prophecy will be fulfilled, and you will be destroyed."

"Silence," screamed One, his cool demeanor abandoning him for the first time, a guard quickly placing his hand forcefully over Seven's mouth. Bean looked at his friend, surprised at her words. Did she now believe in the prophecy, or was this merely a show of bravado? He could sense no deception in her eyes as she glared ferociously at One.

Quickly regaining his composure, One boomed to the crowd, "It looks as if we'll get our money's worth today."

Again the crowd cheered.

"Now, before this traitor so rudely interrupted these fine proceedings, I believe I was about to end the life of the 'Deliverer' and finish this prophecy business once and for all."

One again raised the dagger and moved toward Bean.

This time, from Bean's right, a woman's voice rang out over the top of the wall.

"Stop!"

One instinctively took shelter again in the protection of his robe, expecting another volley of arrows... but none came. One slowly uncovered himself, this time without the dramatic flair. A few murmurs of laughter rose from the crowd, but quickly hushed. One looked rattled. Bean could sense that One knew the overreaction portrayed an unacceptable level of anxiety and weakness in front of his people.

One of the women in white rose from her knees and began to approach the group, but was immediately stopped by the guards. Doing his best to assume a posture of strength once again, One motioned the guards to bring her forward. As she neared the group, Bean strained to make out the face of the woman hidden under the veil.

She knelt before One, laying her cheek on his sandals and pleaded, "Please, oh great One. Please spare his life. I will do whatever you wish. I will fulfill your every want and desire, but please, oh great One, please spare the boy."

With that she sat upright, uncovering her face, looking up at One through tear-filled eyes.

There, before Bean, after all these years - was his sister Katherine.

Chapter 28
Death

"Yes, yes, I was wondering if you were going to just let him die," One said with a sarcastic air. "After all, if it wasn't for your brother, you wouldn't be here - now would you?"

Bean gazed at his sister in amazement. All these years of wondering what had happened to her and now, here she was, standing in front of him. He strained to go to her, but his bindings prohibited it. He was immediately struck by Katherine's youthful appearance. She had vanished when she was 14, but now, six years later, she looked to be no more than 16. Bean remembered what the meek and lowly one had told him about the passage of time in Edinnu.

"Katherine? Is it really you? How did you..."

"Why yes," interjected One impatiently. "It is your sweet sister Katherine. But not to worry, I have taken very, very good care of her. She has quickly become one of my favorites. Not only is she beautiful, but she has a little fire that is quite intoxicating. I must admit, I find a bit of a challenge exhilarating... for a time. Soon she will be of age and I will take her as one of my wives. Yes, yes, it is an honor I bestow only upon the most virtuous and lovely in the Grand Order. As to how your dear sister came to be here," One's voice lowered to almost a whisper, "well, I'm afraid her presence is the result of the rather unfortunate incompetence of my first born. I gave him the simple task of retrieving you. Instead, he panicked and brought back your sister. Sadly, my son is no longer with us. Yes, yes, very tragic indeed. I'm afraid I can't go into the particulars. I'm sure it is for the best though... fathers and sons in my position rarely end well. But that is neither here nor there. Unfortunately, your mother's key stone, which I took such great pains to restore, was good for only one visit to your world in its fractured condition, and I was unable to use it to get back a second time to retrieve you. I vowed then, if given the chance to return, I would send in more trustworthy agents to make sure the job was completed and, to avoid any further mistakes, all of the children in the home would be killed. Yet, somehow you managed to elude my Caretakers. An impressive feat to say the least. But all of that is now water under the bridge as they say, for here you are standing in front of me. I have you, and, as fitting compensation for my considerable time and effort, I have your beautiful sister."

Katherine pleaded, "Tell me what you want Lord and I shall do it. Clearly this little boy is no danger to your majesty and power. Please, use this as an opportunity to show your infinite goodness and mercy to the world."

"No Katherine, don't," Bean interceded. "It's okay, just let him do it. I don't want anyone else to hurt or suffer because of me."

Katherine turned her attention from One and looked at Bean lovingly.

"Every day here I have thought of you, Benjamin. That thought has kept me going. I have longed to see you again, but I prayed with all of my heart it would not be in this place." She paused again as she examined Bean. "You have turned into a very fine young man. Mother and Father must be very proud. I always knew there was something special about you."

"Yes, yes, a touching reunion indeed," interrupted One. "It almost brings a tear to my eye. But alas, we have delayed the proceedings long enough as it is, and this whole affair has become quite tiresome. Yes, yes, quite tiresome indeed. You my love," he said to Katherine dismissively, "will one day give me all that you promise now or your fate will be the same as the boy's mother," motioning toward the ground below where Dawn lay lifeless.

"And as for you," he said, turning to Bean, "unless there are any more women waiting in the wings to try and save you today, the time has come for you to die."

One again approached Bean with the dagger. This time he came very close, putting his left hand behind Bean's back in a disturbing half embrace and carefully placing the tip of the dagger on his chest.

"Please," Bean begged. "Let them go. You have me. You have what you want."

One bent over slightly and whispered into Bean's ear.

"Perhaps I had given you a little too much credit. Clearly you are unaware with whom you are dealing my boy. I have taken your mother from you. Your sister and your friend are now mine to do with as I please. I have taken everything you love from you - now I will take your very life. Oh, and one more thing. In the morning, I will give the order for my armies to destroy every last one of your friends in the Garden. So you see, your bravery and sacrifice will all have been in vain. Just a little something for you to think about as you rot in hell."

With that, Bean felt the point of the dagger pierce his breast. The cold metal of the blade sank into his heart as he felt it beat for the last time. He looked into the horrified eyes of Katherine and Seven... then darkness. He was dead.

Chapter 29
Restoration

Bean struggled to open his eyes. The forest canopy above him was spinning and, for a moment, he thought he might be sick. He quickly closed his eyes again and waited for the nausea to pass. When the spinning diminished, he slowly sat up and took in his surroundings. It appeared he was once again in Edinnu's forest. Instinctively, he felt at his chest. The pain from where he had been stabbed by One was still present, but he felt no wound. Gradually, that pain too subsided, and he stood, looking for Wart or Seven... or anyone. He was alone.

Relief flooded over him as he realized his execution must have been a dream, for it was clear that he was still very much alive. In fact, aside from the initial wooziness, he never felt better. Searching the area for any sign of life, he was struck with an overwhelming urgency compelling him to walk in an eastward direction. As he moved toward the unknown destination, the forest gradually became darker and more overgrown, eventually making it difficult for him to make his way through the dense bushes and trees. Engulfed, he contemplated turning back but knew, for some invisible purpose, he must continue on. After what seemed hours of walking, the forest around him became so dark and foreboding he could only see a few feet in front of him, the foliage so impenetrable that it took a great deal of effort to make even the slightest progress.

Finally, he could go no farther, even though his every desire was to keep moving. He resolved to use all of his remaining energy and will to take just one more step. He reached his hand forward into the darkness only to feel something land on his outstretched fingers. He knew immediately by the texture of the talons on his skin that it was a bird. The bird's touch injected new energy and life into him, and Bean willed himself to take another step forward, and then another, finally finding himself freed from the clutches of the dark forest that now hung like a black curtain behind him.

Observing his new environs, he recognized he was back in the Garden. Looking down at his finger, to his great joy, he saw Maximus gazing up at him with a happy twinkle in his eyes.

"Maximus!" Bean shouted happily, "I thought you were dead!"

"No, no, my boy. As you can see, I am very much alive. It is quite a joy to see you again my friend. I have been waiting for you."

"What happened? I woke up in the forest. I don't know what's real and what's a dream in this place anymore. Where are Wart and Seven and Joshua? Will you take me to the meek and lowly one?"

"There, there. I know you are feeling confused at the moment, but those things are not important now. Be patient, and all of your questions will be answered shortly."

Bean smiled and jabbed at Maximus, "You never were much for giving answers."

Maximus, unoffended, chuckled, "I suppose not. But enough of this tom-foolery. There are others here that long to see you. Shall I take you to them?"

Without waiting for an answer, Maximus turned and flew away, motioning with his wing for Bean to follow.

Traveling for some time across the land, Bean noted this place was identical, in most respects, to that portion of the Garden he had previously visited. However, from time to time they came across large, magnificent buildings made of pure white stone. The structures were more beautiful than any he'd ever seen in his world, and had the most splendid spires on top, seemingly reaching into the heavens. Some reminded him of the pictures of the Taj Mahal he'd seen in Geography class. Passing by several of the buildings, he noted that above the main door of each was placed, in large gold letters, several words written in a strange, foreign language. He wanted to ask Maximus what the words meant, but he could see his diminutive friend was very focused on the two getting to where they needed to be and, true to form, would not easily be distracted by any of his questions.

Bean observed there were many more humans in this part of the Garden, all busily going from one place to another, with most either heading to or away from one of the large buildings. All were dressed in white clothing - the men in pants with buttoned shirts and the women in simple, yet elegant dresses. A few were dressed in long flowing white robes draped over their regular clothing. Bean now, for the first time, realized he was dressed in a similar fashion to those around him. He could not recall changing into this outfit and distinctly remembered being dressed in his pullover when he woke in the forest. Again he wished to ask Maximus about this oddity but his friend remained just out of range to have a conversation. Bean began to think Maximus' distance was intentional to avoid answering just such questions. The people all seemed in too great a hurry to stop and talk with Bean, but not one failed to give a genuine smile and a sincere hello to both he and Maximus as they went by. Many seemed vaguely familiar, but Bean knew there was no way he could have ever met any of them.

After a time, the two approached a small valley filled with a rainbow of beautiful flowers and trees. A small babbling brook meandered through the middle of a golden meadow highlighted by luminescent yellow flowers that seemed to be straining to view their reflection in the running water.

Maximus turned to Bean, "I'm afraid I must leave you now. Just walk that way, and you will find those that await your arrival. I will return soon."

Before he could register any objection, Maximus quickly flew back in the direction they had come, and Bean found himself alone. Slowly turning and walking in the direction Maximus had indicated, he spotted two people in the distance.

Approaching the two figures, he could see a man and woman, walking hand in hand, through the meadow of flowers.

Drawing nearer, it struck Bean that the woman in front of him was his mother, and, though he had never before seen him, he immediately recognized the man as his father. Feelings of love and emotion filled him as he ran to greet them. When they saw him coming, a look of pure delight swept across their faces.

The three embraced and Bean felt himself suddenly being lifted up into his mother's arms. He was amazed that she could lift him as he was already, at his young age, taller than her. Looking down at his arms and legs, he comprehended that his body had miraculously transformed into that of a small baby, no more than a few months old. Rather than shocking him, this radically altered state of being seemed perfectly and utterly natural. His mother cradled him against her chest and began to sing a lullaby as his father tenderly caressed his head. Bean never felt such warmth and safety, and he wished he could remain as a small child in his mother's arms forever.

His father then took him into his arms and began to toss him up into the air. It gave Bean an exhilarating feeling and, as he fell back into his father's hands, he couldn't help but let out a child-like giggle. His father looked so happy to see him, his face so familiar, yet Bean knew it had only been a few moments since he had seen him for the first time.

There, in the Garden with his parents, all time washed away into a glorious whirl of joy and family. In what seemed to Bean to be just a few short hours, he quite literally aged from a small infant into the young man he was today, somehow living an entire childhood, there with his parents, in one afternoon on the meadow. He found he had gained a lifetime of memories and experiences with his father and mother that now equaled those from his youth growing up with his adoptive parents. Somehow, in a brief, beautifully magical period, his parents were finally able to raise the son that they so tragically had to give away, and Bean experienced his youth anew, this time with his true father and mother.

As a warm glow from the setting sun settled across the meadow, Bean gazed at his mother wondering how this all could have happened and if he was merely dreaming. Suddenly, he could hear his mother's voice, though her lips remained still.

"No Benjamin, this is not a dream. This is the most real place of all."

"But how... how could it be?" he thought, not speaking but knowing his mother would hear him.

"You will understand one day. For now, just know that it is part of a great plan of restoration. Restoration of good for good, evil for evil, mercy for mercy, judgment for judgment, justice for justice, hate for hate, charity for charity. You see, all things will be restored to their proper order. And most wonderfully, parents are restored to their children and the children to their parents. Parents who truly love their children and do not have the chance to raise them on earth will have that opportunity here. It is the law of the eternities. It is part of the restoration of beauty for beauty. As you have experienced today, there is nothing in all of heaven and earth that is more beautiful. I honestly believe beauty cannot exist without it."

Before Bean could fully grasp his mother's words, Maximus suddenly reappeared, announcing to the trio, "I'm sorry, but it is time for Benjamin to return."

Bean was puzzled and again spoke aloud.

"Return where? I want to stay here. I want to stay with my parents."

"I understand my boy, but your work is not yet complete. You must return to your body before it is too late."

"My body? I already have a body. Look, I can feel, I can touch, I can move things," he said pleading, as he patted his arms and torso.

"You are in your spirit body. I know it feels the same to you now, but your physical body remains in One City," said Maximus solemnly.

"One City?" said Bean incredulously. His experience with One and his execution in One City was literally a lifetime ago.

Bean turned to his parents, his eyes pleading for them to intervene on his behalf.

Both had a pained, sorrowful look.

"Maximus is right," said his father. "We will be together again soon enough. Until then, you must return. Many are counting on you. Your mother and I have been given a marvelous gift today, but we must now continue our work here. Yours awaits you back in Edinnu."

"I'm not going. I'm staying with you," he stammered defiantly, as tears welled up in his eyes.

His mother caressed his check with the back of her hand as she had done on the wall in One City.

"You must be brave and return. The restoration has only just begun. The gathering is beginning. Your greatest challenges lie ahead. Only if you meet those challenges can you return here with us. You must go back... there is no other way. Your father and I will be close, but you must do this on your own."

With that, his mother and father brought him in for a last embrace. His mother kissed him on the forehead and caressed his check one final time. They then turned and walked away, again hand in hand.

Bean and Maximus made their way back to the forest line in silence. The sun had set long ago and, though no moon was evident in the night sky, Bean had no trouble seeing his surroundings. Finally, as the two approached their final destination, Bean looked at Maximus.

"Is this heaven?" he asked.

Maximus replied, "Not quite, but it is indeed a marvelous place."

"You died that day in the forest, didn't you?"

"Death is a term of such finality. I prefer to say I graduated," Maximus responded.

"Thank you for sacrificing yourself for me. I'm sorry I got you killed," said Bean quietly looking down at the ground.

"You don't remember do you?" said Maximus, puzzled.

"Remember what?"

Maximus now seemed amused, "I guess you haven't been here long enough to remember. Yes, that is only right. Let's simply say I was only returning the favor. Just know that my passing was actually a tremendous blessing to me. As much as I loved those in the Garden, I am now with my family again. I truly have never been happier."

"Are you sure I can't stay?" said Bean again, longingly.

"Nothing would make me happier, but I'm afraid that is impossible. You are needed there. There is no one else to go in your place. There is no other way. You chose this path long ago. You must fulfill what you agreed to do."

Bean furrowed his brow at Maximus' words. He couldn't remember ever agreeing to such a thing, yet could not dispute what his friend was telling him.

"The time has come... you must return now. Until we meet again my friend," Maximus said with a lingering sadness in his voice, motioning to the forest.

Bean walked the thirty or so feet to the forest line. He looked back again at Maximus and the paradise he was leaving behind to return to the nightmare of One City. He turned and stepped into the forest - back into the darkness once again.

Chapter 30
Immortality

Bean opened his eyes to find himself nose to nose with One, who appeared to be in the middle of a thorough examination of his most recent victim. Immediately, Bean was hit with a flash of excruciating pain from where the dagger had just been pulled from his chest. He let out a groan as the agony enveloped his entire body. The physical pain, coupled with an equally unbearable aching to return to the paradise he had just left, was more than his body could take, and he again fell into unconsciousness.

He was brought around again by a sharp slap to the cheek from One, who gripped Bean's face firmly in his hands, examining it for any sign of life. The pain in his chest lessened somewhat, and he slowly opened his eyes. For a brief moment, as Bean looked into the dark eyes of One, he saw reflected a deep and profound fear.

One murmured wondrously, "So it is true. You cannot be killed."

The fear in One's eyes quickly vanished, replaced by... a look of pure delight? One rushed to the edge of the wall yelling exuberantly to the crowd below.

"HE LIVES! THE BOY LIVES!"

The crowd erupted in cheers again, much louder and more robust than before.

Still groggy from his own failed execution, Bean felt shocked and confused by the surprising turn of events. Why was One so pleased that his attempt at murder was unsuccessful? Surely he knew this was a partial fulfillment of the prophecy, the remainder foretelling One's own destruction at Bean's hand. It certainly did not seem to him to be something with which One should be pleased, and yet here he was, literally giddy with excitement.

Adding to the confusion and mental fog, Bean could feel the memory of the time with his mother and father fading from his mind. The more he struggled to hold on to those most precious memories, the more they slipped from his grasp, like grains of sand through his clenched fist. He began to cry knowing that he was losing his parents yet again.

"Bring the boy... and the women," One ordered brusquely as he turned and walked hurriedly toward the guardhouse.

Immediately, Bean was untied and stumbled after One, being dragged on either side by two of the guards. The group made their way down from the wall and across the main plaza towards One's residence, Bean's feet rarely touching the ground. Walking through the pillars and the main door into a palatial entryway, they advanced toward the back of the building until reaching a massive wooden door, latched horizontally with an oaken beam the size of a tree. The door itself was old and unfinished and stood in stark contrast to the new and elaborately decorated walls on either side. It looked as if it had been there long before the palace itself was constructed.

One bellowed for the door to be opened and immediately a company of guards took to either side, hefting the large beam off the latch. As it was laid aside, two guards reached up to grab the large iron handles and began to slowly open the massive structure. The door parted and a wave of sunlight flooded the hall, revealing a small field at the base of the hill rising up from behind the palace.

In contrast to every other inch of Edinnu, the ground in front of the group was barren and dry, with not a single living plant anywhere to be seen. Bean looked up the hill several hundred yards to see the tree he had observed from his room the night before. It was much bigger than he'd remembered, knotted and snarled as if some giant had taken it in his hands and wrung every ounce of life from its trunk. Not a single leaf perched upon any of its branches.

One grabbed Bean gruffly by the back of his neck, moving him forcefully through the doorway. He nodded to two Caretakers and each prodded Seven and Katherine with their razor-sharp antlers to follow. The small group made their way into the field, the door slamming behind them, sending a thunderous boom across the lifeless meadow.

One pushed forward with such vigor that Bean lost his footing and was sent sprawling onto the dry, dusty ground.

"Well, here we are at last," announced One ceremoniously, pacing back and forth in front of Bean. "Yes, yes, the end game, as it were. I must admit I had my doubts about your prophesied immortality my young friend, but I have now witnessed it with my own eyes. I have, with mine own hand, thrust the dagger into your heart. My hands," One said lifting his palms toward Bean, "are covered in your blood. And yet here you are in front of me, very much alive and well. Quite miraculous indeed."

One paused for a moment as if contemplating something singularly magnificent in his mind.

"Don't you see? This is what I have wanted from the beginning. This is all I have ever wanted. Immortality!"

One seemed overwhelmed, his voice now cracking with emotion.

"Why should I, who has done so much for so many and has toiled for so long and hard to achieve such greatness and ascendency, ever have to suffer the ignominy of death? Father Cain yet lives. You say your Jesus Christ yet lives. The three descendants of Joseph yet live. Why, even you, a sniveling little boy, who has done nothing to his credit except to be born, has had bestowed upon him power over that eternal sleep," One said shaking his head in disgust. He continued angrily. "I am the savior of this people! I am the ruler of this world - a world where it was intended for all to live forever. Were it not for the sins of your first parents, I would be immortal. And now you, their precious progeny, are going to make that happen."

"I'm not gonna help you do anything!" Bean shouted defiantly. "You're a mad man. You know now that you can't harm me. You know that the prophecy is true. It's just a matter of time before I destroy you!"

One laughed, "Yes, yes, finally showing a little vim and vigor. Really, it is about time. I was becoming embarrassed for you. But you see, that is precisely why I've brought your two lady friends with us. You have proven your immortality, yes, but I'm fairly certain that your women do not possess a similar immunity from death. As for the prophecy, one thing I've learned is that prophecies are not the defined courses you make them out to be, but are very much dependent on the faithfulness and courage of those about whom such prophecies are made. After spending these past few days with you, I'm more than willing to take my chances. Besides, it will be very difficult for you to destroy me when I myself am immortal."

One bent over and picked Bean up by the chest with one hand, lifting him in the air in front of him.

"Now, listen carefully to me boy. Either you do what I say, exactly as I say it, or I will kill your precious little friend and your dear sweet sister, and I will do it in such horrific fashion that it will haunt you for the rest of your life... which would appear to be a very, very long time."

Bean hesitated, carefully considering One's words.

"No Ben," urged Katherine. "Do not do as he says! You do not know him like I do. We can't let this happen, even if it means our death. You mustn't do it!"

Seven echoed, "Don't do it, Benjamin! We are willing to die! Don't do it."

"Yes, yes, very brave, very brave indeed," snarled One sarcastically. Turning to Bean, he continued. "Perhaps, the death of your mother was not sufficient proof of my dedication to the cause. Perchance your little hunter friend here will help clarify the point."

He grabbed Seven and brought her in front of him with the dagger to her chest. One made a motion as if to slice the dagger across Seven's throat.

"Wait," Bean yelled. "I'll do it." He lowered his head, now almost in a whisper, "Whatever you want... I'll do it."

One released Seven back to the Caretaker.

"Yes, yes, I thought as much. Your weakness sickens me. It is so utterly and completely predictable."

One approached Bean and put his arm around his shoulder, slightly turning him so the pair was facing the hill.

"Now, pay close attention. That tree has cast its shadow over my people long enough," One said pointing toward the top of the hill. "It mocks and taunts me every time I look upon it. What I request of you is really quite simple. You will walk up the hill to the tree, you will pluck a piece of the fruit from the tree - and you will bring it back to me."

Bean was taken aback by the request.

"You want me to pick fruit from the tree? Are you crazy? That tree is dead. There isn't any fruit for me to pick."

"For the sake of these women," One snarled into Bean's ear, "you'd better hope you are wrong. Now move."

Chapter 31
The Tree

The dry, brittle ground crunched beneath his feet as Bean began his walk up the hillside, noticing for the first time a scattering of bones and various types and pieces of armor on the ground around him. The higher he progressed, the more evidence of carnage he encountered, requiring him to step gingerly at times to avoid stepping on any remains. It was clear to him he was not the first person to make the journey up the hill, and it was evident that few, if any, who started the journey, finished it.

The clouds grew more dark and ominous with each step, and an unearthly glow began to creep over the entire area. Half way up the hill, the evidence of death and destruction gradually waned and the grass around him inexplicably began to green, the hillside suddenly taking bloom in front of his eyes. Now, looking up at the tree, he saw beautiful massive leaves literally springing forth from the branches. The boughs began to sag from the weight of the fruit that erupted from the limbs.

Bean stopped for a moment to take in the beauty of the tree. It now seemed three to four times larger than the dead, gnarled tree he had viewed from the bottom of the hill just a few minutes before. He stood in wonder, finding within him a growing desire to get to the tree and eat a piece of the fruit. Just looking at it, he knew its taste would surpass anything he had ever eaten, and he longed with everything in him to partake.

He now set off quicker than before. The clouds continued to worsen and began to spin like the ominous tornado cells Bean had seen a time or two back home in Missouri. The gusting wind began to make his progress more difficult. He looked at the tree to find its appearance had changed yet again. The leaves and fruit began to take on a golden glow and, as he neared, the tree looked to have actually taken fire. In front of him now was the very image he had seen from his balcony the night before. His desire to get to the tree and eat the fruit was now gone - replaced by fear. He turned around, looking for Seven and Katherine, barely making out their forms through the inclement weather that was worsening by the second. Regaining his resolve, he knew there was no other option but to keep moving forward.

Just as the wind began to completely overpower him, Bean managed one final step and suddenly found himself in what appeared to be the eye of the storm. Immediately, sunlight flooded the area and Bean, squinting, looked up to see the clear blue sky above him. Taking in his newly altered surroundings, he could now make out three forms standing between him and the tree. As he neared, he could see the beings were the three women he had seen the previous evening.

Seemingly oblivious to his presence to this point, the three women now took note of his company, slowly turning their heads toward him in unison. He was at first taken aback by the stark beauty of the women. Their bright red flowing hair seemed blown by the wind even though the air was now perfectly still. Their alabaster skin emitted an eerily luminescent glow. Each wore a long white robe matching the brightness of the leaves on the tree. Their arms and legs were bare just below the elbows and knees, and he noticed the women's feet did not touch the ground, instead floating a few inches in the air.

Bean immediately felt uncomfortable under the weight of their stares and was unable to match their gaze for more than a moment. Not sure how to proceed, he finally worked up the courage to again move towards the women. Upon doing so, their countenances suddenly became stern and angry. In a flash, their robes changed from white to blood red, their flaming red hair igniting into bright white flames. Battling every instinct to turn and run, Bean forced himself to move forward. The women began to elevate high off the ground, their faces morphing into a frighteningly grotesque nightmare, their once perfect teeth swelling into horribly misshapen fangs. Their fingers extended into long, thin, skeletonish extremities finishing in razor sharp claws. Each released an agonizing and terrifying groan as massive wings ripped through the flesh on their backs and unfurled five feet on either side of the creatures. A rush of air blew against his face as the wings began to move up and down and the three began to fly rapidly in a circle around him. The scene was now more than Bean could take and he fell to the earth, covering his head with his arms in an attempt to shield himself from an imminent attack from the frightening beings.

From above came the voices of the women in unison, sounding like a waterfall crashing against the rocks below and penetrating him to the very core.

"We are Cherubim. Who dares approach the Tree of Life?"

Bean answered meekly, "I mean no harm. I must get a piece of fruit from the tree."

The Cherubim thundered, "No one shall partake of the fruit of the Tree of Life. We are charged to guard and protect the Tree, lest those who partake live forever and become as God. Only those with the correct name and emblem may draw nigh unto the Tree of Life."

"Who dares approach the Tree of Life?" the Cherubim demanded again.

Bean managed to rise.

"My name is Ben Greene," he said, attempting to sound confident... then remembering, added, "Benjamin James Greene."

The Cherubim swirled around, slowly descending upon him. Bean struggled to keep his eyes open; the grotesque visages more frightening than anything he could have ever imagined. One of the Cherubim was now directly in front of him, just a few inches from his face. The other two positioned themselves on either side, equally close. He felt as if he could bear it no longer and that he would perish under the weight of his own fear. He closed his eyes, awaiting his utter destruction. Finally, the Cherubim said in harmony.

"We know you, Benjamin."

Surprised at the sudden change of tone in the Cherubim's voices, Bean allowed himself to squint through his closed eyelids. To his great relief, the Cherubim had once again returned to their original form, their initial beauty fully restored.

"Do you have the emblem?" they asked.

Bean was at a loss. He had no emblem. He was not even sure he knew what an emblem was. He had nothing with him but the clothes on his back. He fumbled around his clothing, searching for something, anything. Catching his attention was what he did not find – the key stone. He carried it with him everywhere he went, but he'd left it back in the Garden. The key stone must be the emblem, he thought, his disappointment palpable as it would be of no use to him now.

Bean looked down, "I have nothing. I only have myself."

Again in unison, the Cherubim spoke, "Without the emblem, you cannot pass."

"Please," Bean pleaded earnestly, "I must have a piece of fruit from the tree."

The Cherubim repeated firmly, "Without the emblem, you cannot pass."

Bean again felt at his clothing, searching for anything else that could be the emblem. As he patted his chest, he winced from the pain of the open wound where One had moments ago plunged the dagger. Gently pressing against the injury with his fingers, he sensed the presence of his mother, again whispering the words she had recited to him that first night in his room.

"Sacrifice is a sign of worthiness."

The faint whisper melted into nothingness and the realization came upon Bean that he had been willing to give his very life to protect his family and friends. It was the ultimate sacrifice he could have made for them. Gently he pulled back his clothing to reveal the fresh laceration on his chest.

The Cherubim drew close again, each reaching their hands inside his garment to softly caress the gash. Bean braced for the pain but none came, even when the Cherubim inserted their hands into the depth of the wound.

Slowly they stood back and, in accord, spoke solemnly, "This is the emblem. You may pass."

The Cherubim then returned to their original positions, bowed their heads, closed their eyes and placed their palms together as if once again in prayer.

His path now clear of the Cherubim, Bean approached the tree but quickly discovered there still remained a significant obstacle in accomplishing his objective.

In front of the tree was an immense sword of fire, rotating wildly in the air directly in his path. He initially tried to make his way around it, but discovered any attempt to do so was in vain, as the sword would move to block any available route to the tree.

He had made it this far, he thought, could this be the end now? Bean watched the razor sharp edges of the fiery blade rotate before him with such speed that there was no hope he could grasp the sword without being severely injured, or killed. Even if he could clutch the sword, the fire engulfing the weapon would surely make holding it, even for a fraction of a second, impossible. Not knowing what else to do, he pleaded for help from his mother.

"I know you are here with me. Please tell me what to do."

There was no whisper this time. In desperation, he began to recite his mother's words again:

"Benjamin, before you were, you were chosen. Your destiny and our fate have forever been one. Seek the noble and great, for your mission is not yours alone. Sacrifice is the truest sign of worthiness. Reach into the darkness and you will seize the light."

"That's it," he murmured, slowly repeating the last line. "Reach into the darkness and you will seize the light."

He closed his eyes, repeating the words yet again.

"Reach into the darkness..."

A feeling of peace now swept over him. He slowly began to reach his arm toward the sword. He could feel the scorching heat from the blade on his fingers and hesitated for a moment. Thoughts of Katherine and Seven again flooded his mind. He knew there was no turning back, that there was no other way. Regaining his resolve, he forcefully thrust his arm toward the sword. His hand erupted in pain, and he could not be sure if it was burning or if it had been cut off completely. With every ounce of strength remaining, he thrust his hand further and suddenly felt the hot metal of the sword's hilt. Quickly gripping it with his hand, he opened his eyes to find himself holding the massive flaming sword in front of him.

The pain in his hand was replaced with a surge of power and energy that rushed down his arm and into his entire body, giving him a feeling of strength and invincibility. Looking in awe at the massive weapon ablaze before him, he wanted to shout in triumph, but no words could escape his mouth. Given its size, he should not be capable of hoisting the sword with both hands, let alone one, but he was able to hold it and wield it in front of him as if it was one of the fake paper swords he used to make as a boy.

With sword in hand, Bean's attention now turned to the tree itself. Its branches looming above, he was finally able to see the fruit in detail. It was surprisingly plain compared to most of the other fruit he had encountered in the Garden. Its shape was a mix of an apple and a pear and the surface had the texture of a plum. Despite its plainness, the color made it utterly magnificent. It looked golden from afar, but now, up close, it was the purest and most brilliant white Bean had ever seen.

He hesitated for a moment, not wanting to mar the perfection of the fruit, then reached to grab a piece from one of the lower branches, plucking it gently from the tree. He gazed at it, bewildered, its beauty nothing short of hypnotic. His desire to bite into it was greater than he had ever felt for anything in his life. His arm tensed as he fought to restrain himself, only the thought of Katherine and Seven gave him the will to resist.

And so there stood Bean atop the hill, flaming sword in his right hand and a fruit from the Tree of Life in his left. He extended his arms, tilting his face towards the sky, basking in the triumphant sunlight. He had done it. He had accomplished a seemingly impossible task. For a moment, he was invulnerable. For a moment, he was everything he ever dreamed of being. For a moment, he was truly happy.

A sharp thunder clap rattled him from his euphoria, reminding him of the dark, turbulent clouds that still encircled below. Bean staggered, the rush of power from the sword suddenly fading, his newfound strength swept away by a flash flood of doubt. An onslaught of questions fired within his mind. "How can this be?" he thought. "How could this happen – to me? I am nothing... I am nobody. What good does this do anyway? I'd be better off dying up here. If One gets a hold of this fruit, that will be the end for everyone."

Bean's fleeting moment of peace and clarity crumbled under the task that still laid ahead, a task he knew would be the most difficult of all.

Lowering his head, he somberly turned to walk back down the hill.

Chapter 32
Truth

Bean neared the small group. Seeing the sword, One quickly stepped to the side and grabbed Katherine, bringing her in front of him and raising the dagger to her neck.

"If you value the life of your sister, you will be very cautious with that sword."

Bean slowed his walk, extending the sword to his side in a position of submission. Quickly ascertaining Bean would not risk hurting his sister, One changed to a more pleasant tone.

"Yes, yes, I must admit, I didn't have much hope of you returning with the fruit. I assumed you would be killed like all the others, which would have been a favorable result for me regardless. But here you are, with fruit in hand, a much more pleasant outcome for all of us I should think. Yes, yes, a most impressive feat. You continue to best my expectations for you, meager though they may be."

One moved forward slightly, carefully positioning Katherine between himself and the sword.

"Now, my boy," One paused for dramatic effect, reaching towards Bean, "deliver the fruit to me. My immortality is at hand!"

Katherine spoke tenderly, "Ben, I want you to listen to me. Do not give him that fruit. The consequences would be devastating and eternal. Take no thought of me... I am a True Believer. I am not afraid of death. I am ready."

One pressed the dagger against Katherine's throat and a slight trickle of blood rolled down her neck.

"You will be silent or I shall silence you forever," One said angrily.

Snapping back to Bean, One continued with heightened ferocity.

"Yes, yes, mighty Deliverer. Kill your own sister if you will. But know this, if you kill me, One Caretaker here will slaughter your little friend before I hit the ground. And if that doesn't provide sufficient motivation for you, you should know I've instructed my other Caretakers, in the event of my untimely demise at your hand, to find your little brother and end him as well. I believe you are already familiar with their unique dedication to a task, no?" One hesitated, allowing his words to fully sink in.

"Yes, yes, I know all about your repulsive little brother. I'd be doing you a favor with that one, I should think," One said, shaking his head in disgust.

"So, what is it to be? Yes, yes, a very difficult decision indeed. All the many sacrifices made and pains endured to protect your loved ones. Are you going to be responsible for their destruction now?"

"Don't listen to him Ben," yelled Seven. "End him, end him now! I am not afraid. You *are* the Deliverer. I believe in you. I believe in it all. End him!"

Seven felt the tip of the Caretaker's horn against her back puncture her skin, and she winced in pain.

Bean stood silently, taking in the scene in front of him. The magical time with his mother and father but a few hours earlier had now vanished from his memory, yet he was left with an undeniable impression that death was not the end. He believed Katherine and Seven would live on, even if One carried through on his threats. Yet, how could he be responsible - how could he bring such pain upon them? How could he live with himself if he did not do everything in his power to protect them? He was willing to die for them, but he was not willing to let them die for him. Dropping the tip of the sword to the ground, he looked down in hopelessness, the flame now almost extinguished.

"I'm sorry - I can't. I just can't do it."

Bean knew he had lost. Perhaps One did not have the power to kill him, but he could easily lock Bean away in prison for the rest of his life, however long that might be. And it was now clear that his immortality did not render him impervious to pain or injury. One certainly had the tools at his disposal to make his immortality a curse rather than a blessing.

And what would become of Katherine and Seven? Perhaps their death would be a blessing, knowing what life with One would mean after this. He had let them down, he knew that, and though they were disappointed in him now, that disappointment would one day turn to contempt and even hatred as they would be forced to endure a lifetime of misery.

Bean thought of the disillusionment of Joshua and the meek and lowly one. It was clear now he was not the Chosen One or the Deliverer. They had placed all of their hopes on him. They were willing to sacrifice everything. Yet he was what he knew himself to be all along - a scared, worthless little boy. He had tried to tell them, but they wouldn't listen. Eventually One's forces would be victorious and all his friends in the Garden would be dead. And for what reason... because of his weakness and cowardice.

His thoughts turned to Warren. He had left him behind, all alone in a strange world. He had promised him everything would be alright, but he knew One would never stop until Warren was dead. He had always failed as a brother and now, the ultimate failure. He alone would be responsible for his brother's murder.

Finally, Bean's mind drifted to that day with his father as they stood together in the field looking at the crumbled wall. He had asked Bean to help him heal the family... and he had promised his father he would. And now - now he had destroyed everything. His parents would be condemned to live the rest of their lives in pure hell, not knowing what had happened to their children. And it was all his fault - everything was his fault.

In utter dejection, Bean looked down at the ground as he began to lift the fruit towards One. Reaching it forward,

Bean's eyes drifted to the now smoldering sword. With the fire diminished, he could make out, etched in bold capital letters along the blade, the word "JUSTICE."

"The Sword of Justice," whispered Bean in wonderment, unconsciously pulling back the fruit from One's outstretched fingers.

"The Sword of Justice," he muttered softly again.

One reacted angrily, "That is enough! My patience is at an end. Give me the fruit or your sister dies this instant!"

Bean looked up at One, then to Katherine and finally to Seven. He saw the fire in her eyes as she mouthed the words, "I believe."

Finally, he looked again at One. Bean could feel his very soul well up within him. His entire body became warm, his heart burning as if it, like the sword he held in his hand, was on fire. He again hefted the sword in the air, now fully ablaze. It was now clear what he must do – what he was destined to do.

He drew back the sword, yelling with a might and force that reverberated across the land.

"JUSTICE DESTROYS ONLY THE WICKED!"

Bean sent the flaming sword slicing through the air towards Katherine and One, striking them both through their midsections. As the sword fell on him, One let out an agonizing shriek. A bolt of lightning exploded from One's chest that leapt to the tree atop the hill, then fractured into thousands of bolts shooting upwards from its branches and filling the sky. In an instant, One's ashy skin blackened, then split allowing hot lava to explode through the cracks. For the briefest of moments, the eyes of reluctant Deliverer and self-proclaimed Savior met. Bean could see One's pure hatred melt into the fear of a damned soul, then give way to the lava bursting forth from One's eye sockets. Before the sword could make its way completely through One's torso, his body was already consumed by fire, and One collapsed to the earth in a smoldering mound of blackness.

The sword continued on its path, cutting through both Seven and One Caretaker, splitting the animal in two and killing it before it could make a sound.

The force of the swing spun Bean around, away from Katherine and Seven, before he could stop his momentum. Fearing the worst, he slowly turned to face them. There before him stood Katherine and Seven, unhurt by the sword passing through them. For a moment, the group remained breathless, dumbstruck by the wonder of the last few seconds. Finally, Seven screamed, "You did it! You did it, Ben!" and the three came together in an exultant embrace.

The remaining Caretaker, upon seeing One and his brother slain in front of him, quickly turned and ran up the hill in fear. As it neared the tree, one of the Cherubim pounced upon it, savagely tearing it to pieces. The other two Cherubim descended from the hilltop and alit in front of the group. One of them approached Bean and said solemnly, with hand outstretched, "None shall partake of the fruit."

Bean immediately offered it up, the Cherubim parting the front of her robe and placing it within her bosom, the fruit fusing with her body until it disappeared completely. The other Cherubim quickly retrieved the sword from the ground where Bean had dropped it and returned it back to its place in front of the tree.

Finally, the Cherubim who had taken the fruit spoke to the group.

"It is still not safe for you in this place. There remain many that seek your destruction. We will take you to your friends in the Garden."

With that, the Cherubim took Bean, Katherine and Seven into their arms, unfurled their wings, and ascended up into the sky.

Chapter 33
Joy

It was roughly a two-day journey to the northeastern end of Edinnu where Bean's wall and the entry back into his world were located. He had already said his goodbyes to the meek and lowly one.

The situation remained unstable between the True Believers and the inhabitants of the Seven Cities, but with the death of One, the forces amassed at the forest edge had retreated, and there was no longer any immediate threat. Bean had initially offered to stay in the Garden, but the meek and lowly one told him they could handle whatever was to come, that his work in the Garden was done for now, and it was time for Bean to return home to his mother and father.

Wart, Katherine, Seven, Joshua, Ronar and Baffus accompanied Bean to the wall. He still couldn't quite grasp why they weren't returning to the place where he and Wart initially entered Edinnu, though Joshua had tried to explain several times that, even though there was only one wall, the entry was not the exit. It hurt Bean's mind to think about it for too long, so he simply added it to the long list of things about the Garden of Eden he knew he would never fully understand.

Bean recognized the wall immediately as the group approached. He was intimately familiar with the stone structure, having spent the entirety of the summer building it. Yet, it remained an eerie feeling to see the wall and not be able to see his home on the other side. The hodgepodge company came to a halt just shy of the rocks. Bean knew the time had now come to say goodbye to Joshua and Seven.

Joshua approached in his usual affable manner, arms outstretched with a smile stretching from ear to ear. He lifted Bean off the ground with a giant bear hug and then, after depositing him back upon the earth, brusquely grabbed Bean's face between his hands.

"From the first moment I saw you, I saw greatness. I never doubted you for a moment. You have been our deliverer in more ways than one. I shall miss you greatly, my friend."

Joshua kissed him firmly on the cheek then finally released Bean's face from his hands. Blushing, Bean replied, "Thank you Joshua. Thank you for believing in me. I will miss you too... very much."

Glancing to his left, Bean smiled as he saw Wart kneeling on the ground, his arms clinging to Baffus' neck, his back heaving up and down in great sobs. Bean never imagined he'd see a warthog in tears, but it was clear Baffus was equally distraught that he was losing his best friend. Wart pleaded with Baffus to come with him, but Baffus sadly explained he was needed in the Garden for now. He tried to comfort Wart by telling him they would see each other again someday, and that their friendship would last forever.

Bean knew it was now time for the moment he'd dreaded for the past two days. He must say goodbye to Seven. She quietly walked up to him and took him by the hand, leading him to a secluded area away from the rest of the group, her grip so firm it almost caused him pain.

Finally alone, she mercifully released his hand and took Bean into her arms. With her mouth next to his ear, she whispered intently.

"Before you, I didn't think I would ever care about anyone or anything again. You've changed my world. I feel alive for the first time, and yet right now... I feel like I'm about to die. I can't bear to lose you," she quivered, breaking into tears.

He could feel the moisture as she brought her cheek next to his.

Bean had practiced a speech, but his mind was now blank.

"Come with us," was all he could muster. "Come with me."

"I want to go with you," Seven said earnestly. "But, this is my home. Just as you need to go back to your home, I must stay in mine. I love Joshua like a father. I can't begin to tell you the sacrifices he's made to keep me with him in Seven City. I can't leave him alone here now. He lost his entire family in the Great Battle. I'm all he has left. I just can't leave him."

Pausing for a moment, she continued with a wry smile, "Besides, what would the True Believers do without their best archer?"

The two broke their embrace, their hands now intertwined at their sides.

"I will think of you every day," said Seven.

She leaned in and gave Bean a sublimely soft and gentle kiss just to the side of his mouth, their lips missing by the breadth of a butterfly's wing.

Bean's legs waivered as a surge of excitement washed over his body, more powerful than when he grasped the Sword of Justice for the first time. He was again left speechless. After a moment, he regained a small degree of composure.

"I'll come back for you," he said with all the earnestness he could muster.

Seven grinned slightly, looking to the ground. Finally, the two turned hand in hand and walked back to rejoin the group.

The kiss set Bean's mind awhirl. Lost in the fog of love that now enveloped him, a small movement from the forest suddenly caught his eye. Straining to make out the source, his breath was taken as he thought he saw the dark, hulking silhouette of Mahan retreating into the blackness of the trees. In a blink he was gone. Seven, sensing the change in mood, asked Bean what was the matter.

After a few seconds, he simply said, "Oh, I think I'm just imagining things. I guess your kisses are pretty powerful," he laughed. "I'm sure it's nothing."

Upon returning to the wall, Bean retrieved the key stone from his pocket. The meek and lowly one had returned it to him upon his reappearance at the Garden and told Bean it was now his to do with as he wished. He could feel the energy from the stone in his hands grow with its proximity to the wall. As he laid it on the rocks, as he had done weeks ago, in front of him opened the familiar scene of the field leading to his home. Gazing at his house once again, he realized, for the first time since he'd left, just how desperately he longed to return there.

Bean turned back and reached his hand to Katherine, helping her climb over the wall. Next, he lifted his brother to the top of the wall, and Wart jumped off onto the other side. Finally, he straddled his long legs one by one until he was standing on the other side as well. The two groups looked sorrowfully at each other across the wall. Bean wondered if he would ever see his friends again... if he would ever see

Seven again. Their eyes locked one final time as Bean slowly retrieved the key stone. As the stone lifted, he saw a small tear drop from Seven's cheek. Before it could hit the ground, Seven had disappeared into the familiar forest.

The three stood there quietly for a moment. Finally Katherine walked over to Bean and grasped his hand. She took Wart by her other hand, and they turned to cross the field back to their home. About half way across the meadow, a low shout rang from inside the house, followed immediately by his father bursting out the back door in a dead run towards the children, hooting and hollering. Before his dad could reach them, a slight flutter caught Bean's eye from the kitchen window. He could see the face of his mother as she pulled back the curtains. For a moment she seemed confused, and then, finally... Bean saw pure joy.

End of Book One

About the Author

Mark Durrant is a practicing attorney and radio broadcaster living in Salt Lake City, Utah. Mark is married to Marilee and is the father of four children - George, Jordan, Dane and Stratton. This is his first novel. Look for Mark on Facebook (www.facebook.com/mark.durrant.52) and on Twitter (@DurrantMark).

Made in the USA
Middletown, DE
19 December 2017